The Incarnations of Mariela Peña

First published in Great Britain in 2021 by Black Shuck Books

Cover design by WHITEspace
from "Memory"
by Elihu Vedder
Courtesy of the Los Angeles County Museum of Art

Set in Caslon by WHITEspace
www.white-space.uk

978-1-913038-66-3

The Incarnations
of Mariela Peña

by
Steven J Dines

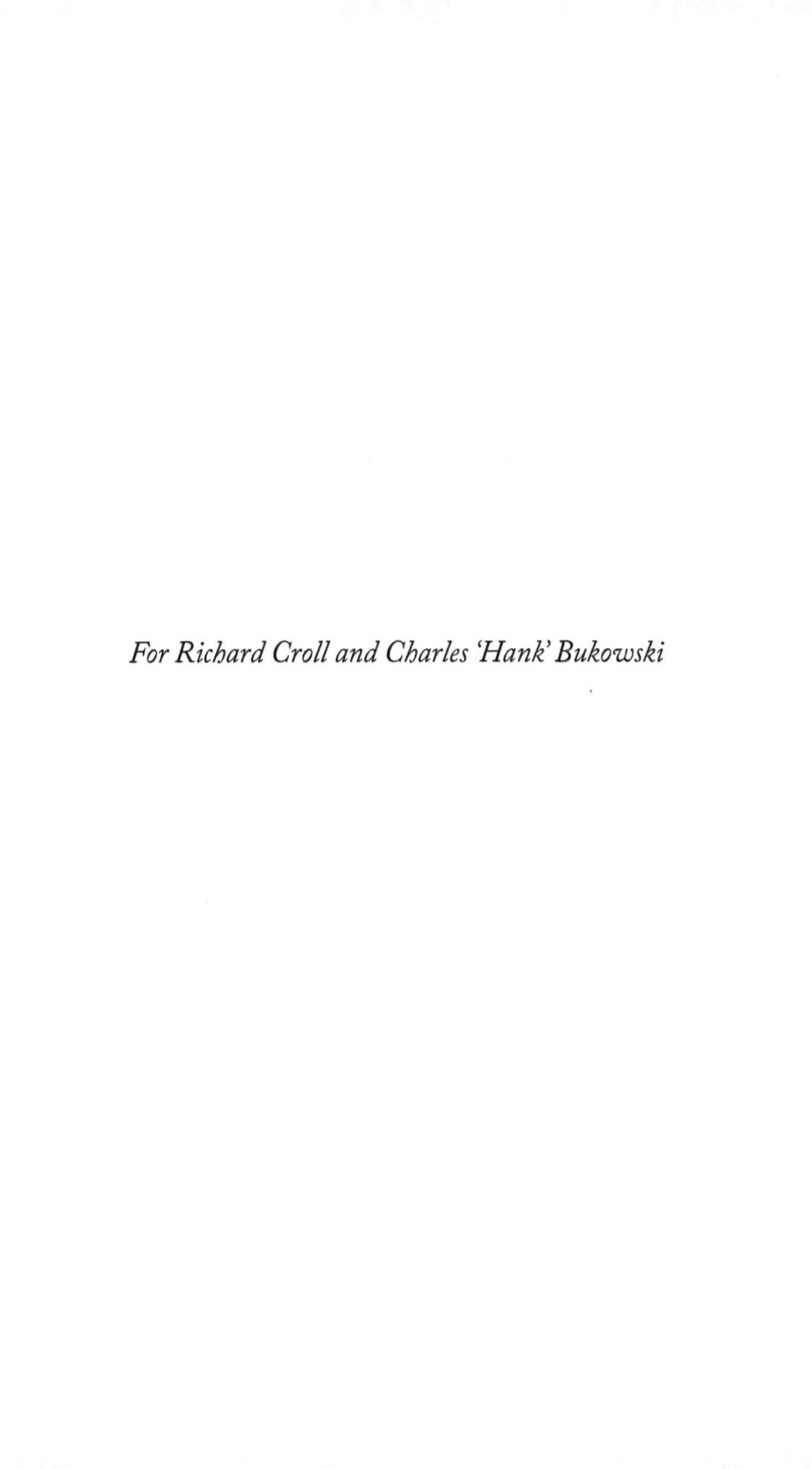

For Richard Croll and Charles 'Hank' Bukowski

The past is never dead

—William Faulkner

Infected

They sat on a beach in Libya and listened to the surf. Foster focussed on the breakers, something climactic and loud; Poet on each dying wave as it retreated across the shore, rattling pebbles in its wake with a sound like grinding teeth. Then came the lull, the hush between one wave and the next, like an intake of breath. Foster sat up straight, glanced at the tactical rifle at his side, wondered – not for the first time – what the Mediterranean might throw at them next. Poet closed his eyes and remembered the time in Mexico when he had gone base jumping with Mariela into the Cave of the Swallows, how the only sound then had been the air rushing past his ears at fifty feet per second. For him, now, the silence was just that – a freefall: the pucker before the kiss. Waves had to break, chutes had to open, lips had to meet before you felt truly alive. Otherwise, there was *only* freefall. Silence. Death.

No.

Not even that.

Not anymore.

"Heads up," Foster said. "Tourist. Three o'clock."

Poet's eyes snapped open and he glanced to his right at the corpulent figure staggering out of the sea onto the beach three hundred feet east of where the two men sat.

White male, long khaki shorts, white socks, sneakers, the kind of shirt you only ever wore on vacation.

Foster stood. Raised his rifle. Peered through the scope. The tourist's standard-issue straw hat was probably afloat somewhere on the Med, along with the better part of his insides. The scope's crosshairs centred on a beach-ball-sized cavity in his otherwise fleshy stomach. A couple of small fish were flopping around inside the wet, glistening hole, eating or trying to breathe, Foster could not tell. He lowered his rifle, did a three-sixty neck roll, raised the weapon, aimed, fired.

The tourist fell, the part of him that had chosen to wear the fugly shirt spraying a spectacular dark fan behind him.

Poet looked at the ground between his feet and sighed.

Foster sat on a rock. Leaned his rifle against another.

"Next one is yours."

Poet did not look up, only raised his bandaged hand in mute reply.

"Hey, we have our orders," Foster said. "Nobody gets on those islands, nobody gets off."

One month ago, Malta and Gozo had been declared a quarantine zone by the World Health Organization. What some were calling an outbreak and others – conspiracy theorists – were calling Operation Julius had infected up to one million people at the height of the summer tourist season. A small fraction, maybe less than point zero five per cent, were believed to be part of some IS offshoot operating out of the Middle East, trying to infiltrate Europe under the guise of asylum seekers. Libya had been their gateway to the north, one of many, but they had not bargained on the gate being slammed in their face the moment they set foot on European soil. The debate over who had done the slamming currently raged throughout the rest of Europe, with the West and Kiev pointing fingers squarely at their old enemy, the Russians.

"You really think it's possible to contain that many people – or that none of them will make it out?" Poet picked up a handful of hot sand and watched the grains slip through his fingers. "NATO can't put troops on every inch of Mediterranean coastline. They simply don't have the numbers. Shit, they can't even return our calls."

"I don't know about the other beaches," Foster said. "All I know about is this one. It's clean, and on my watch it's gonna *stay* clean."

"We should bail," Poet said. "Head south to Al Bayda. Anywhere there's people. We need to find out what the hell is going on."

"Let's just sit tight for now," Foster said. "Keep trying the radio. We have food and water and these incredible views. This is an easy detail, Corporal. In fact, this might be as good as it gets for anybody right now."

Poet knew it was hopeless. If the world had gone Tango Uniform then Foster did not want to know. He was frightened and inflexible. But Poet had to try something. He had to get away from this beach, and not just because their supplies were running low.

"We'll be black on water in six days, sir."

"Then talk to me in five. For now, we stay. We take out the trash. We bury the trash. Until our CO or God tells us otherwise."

Poet said nothing more, nor had he lifted his gaze during the entire conversation. He had neither the energy nor the desire to look up and see this trigger-happy son of a bitch haloed by the sun. No, siree.

Besides, there was blood and pus seeping through the bandage on his left hand. A dime-sized spot for now, but he would need to change the dressing before long. Of greater concern, though, was the sensation in his hand and now his wrist: an itch just about everywhere below the epidermis. Maddening as hell.

"I'm heading back to the caves," he said, standing to stretch his limbs in readiness for the short hike into the forested lower foothills of the Jebel Akhdar. "This heat is making me nauseous, and my hand hurts."

Foster shook his head as he gazed out to sea.

"What?" Poet asked.

"Nothing."

"You got something to say, sir – say it."

Foster stood up quickly. "Alright, I will. Get over her."

"Who?"

"You know damn well. The girl from yesterday."

"You don't know what you're talking about, sir."

"Bullshit. Of course this is about her. You put a bullet through some kid's skull and that's a step too far for you. So you cut your own hand to make it look like you can't use your weapon—"

"That's not what happened."

"Whatever. Look, I get it, Poet. I do. Just don't *lie* to me about it, that's all I'm saying."

"She couldn't have been older than fifteen," Poet said. Without Foster seeing, he held his bandaged palm between the thumb and finger of his right hand and squeezed hard. The pain flared up his arm like napalm and reached inside his chest with its fiery grip. "I didn't sign up for this."

"Kid was already dead," Foster said. "She just didn't know it yet. None of them do. We can't let them carry the infection off those rocks—" he jabbed a finger northwest, toward Malta and its sibling islands "—onto the mainland."

"Tell me something," Poet said. "How much of the Libyan coast did they hand over to us to patrol?"

"About three klicks. Why?"

"And how many low-rank Army Reserve schmucks like us do you think will be guarding the coast of Sicily tonight? Or patrolling some stretch of southern France? Two, like us?"

"What's your fucking point, Corporal?"

Poet sighed, then looked up. Foster had maybe ten years on him; he was pushing forty, and forty was pushing back. But what had he done with those extra years?

Worked on his winning personality, Poet thought.

"NATO doesn't care about protecting this beach," he said. "Or this country. Or any of the Middle East for that matter. They'll gladly sit on their hands and let this virus take out the whole region, at which point they'll swoop in for the oil or fight the Russians for it, who, by the way, want Julius to do what he does best."

"Enough with the bullshit theories."

"*Divida et Impera*, Foster. Divide and rule. It wouldn't surprise me one bit if they were behind the whole sorry mess. Them or the Syrians. They've been pretty tight throughout this whole thing."

Foster thrust a palm at Poet's face. "I said enough. You shot some kid and because you can't deal with it you want to stand here and discuss conspiracies all day. Not gonna happen. Embrace the suck. Move the hell on."

"What if you're wrong?"

Foster lowered his hand. "About what, the Russians?"

"No – them. What if they know they're dead? What if they still feel…I don't know, *something*."

Foster shrugged. "Then you did that girl a huge fucking favour, son. Probably thank you for it too."

"If she could."

"That's right. If she could."

They stood and eyeballed each other in the oppressive heat. It was late afternoon but it would remain hot long into the night. For Foster, this was about the heat and Poet's reluctance to admit the truth about the cut on his hand. For Poet, it was about the heat, the girl, the heat, but mostly the girl.

Someone's daughter.

Someone's sister.

Someone's *someone*.

Sweat trickled down the faces of both men.

Something drew Foster's attention. He glanced across Poet's shoulder. When he looked at Poet again, he was grinning.

"You're up," he said with a nod in the other direction.

Poet gave in and turned around.

"Holy shit," he said in a low voice. "Is that…"

"Indeed it is," Foster replied.

Like the tourist earlier, he emerged from the sea staggering and stumbling like he had gone for a long swim and struck his head on a rock. Unlike the tourist, he looked mostly intact after the three-hundred-mile trek across the seabed behind him, although dressed as he was from head to toe in black robes, with the merest slit for his eyes, it was hard to tell what putrefaction dripped underneath.

Side by side, the two soldiers watched the undead terrorist's movements. For several minutes, he lurched in a wide circle, head bowed, fixed only on the ground directly in front of his feet. Slowly, he carved a deepening groove through his own footprints in the sand, locked in his own circuitous path, unable to break free of it until eventually he stumbled and fell, out of the circle, out of the spell.

Foster broke the silence with his loud, raucous laugh.

It was the kind of laugh that drew too much attention to itself, Poet thought. He pictured a crowded elevator stopping on some floor of a burning building and everyone inside pushing to get out. He asked Foster if he felt okay.

"Hell yeah," came the reply. "Look at that fucking thing. It's goddamn hilarious." He laughed again, the sound falling over itself to get out.

He's dangerous, Poet thought. *And not just to them.*

He turned his attention back to the figure on the beach. He had seen the pictures and watched the videos posted on the internet of the beheadings and the shootings, of men's bodies hanging over the entrances to terrorist-occupied districts, of heads displayed on railings, but this was the first time he had ever encountered one of the perpetrators of those crimes in the flesh. Evidently, this one had abandoned the guise of the asylum seeker and returned to traditional garb, which begged the question: what the blue fuck had been happening or about to happen on Malta and Gozo in the hours before Julius was dropped?

The thought made Poet feel numb all over, except for that hateful itch underneath the dressing on his hand. The wound screamed, and it took nearly everything he had not to prise it open and go digging around in there with the fingers of his good hand.

Foster was silent now. He stood watching the terrorist, who was on his feet again and wandering along the beach, away from the two soldiers. Poet was surprised he had not heard Foster laughing and turned in their direction. Foster, on the other hand, was disappointed it hadn't; a bullet through the back of the skull from range was almost too good for it, he felt. This one should be up close and personal. Both men squinted against the sunlight and watched.

From a distance of four hundred feet, heat haze rising all around him from a billion grains of superheated sand, the man in black took on an unreal, almost mythical quality.

Here was a monster from twenty-first-century legend.

"End the son-of-a-bitch," Foster growled.

Poet looked down and saw his tactical rifle thrust into his hands. Still disorientated, he stared at it as though it was some strange object he had just found washed up on the beach.

"One shot, right here," Foster said, tapping the base of his own skull. "Take the head clean off. Even with your hand the way it is, that shouldn't be a problem."

"I'm not sure I—"

"Make it clean and it won't even know it's gone. Not right away. Ten bucks says you make that shot, that thing takes as many steps before it realises and drops. That's a dollar a step. What do you say?"

"I don't know..."

"Take the shot."

"I—"

"Take the shot. Come on. These pig fuckers take our boys' heads, we take theirs."

And there's the rub, Poet thought.

"Do not get sentimental on me, asshole. What are you waiting for?" Colour was rising through Foster's face now, matching the rise in volume of his voice. "Wax that fucker, *now*. Take the shot. Poet, take the shot. Jesus H. Christ…if you can shoot some little girl, you can do this motherfucker all day long. Now, take the goddamn shot, Corporal!"

Poet lowered the rifle to his side. He shook his head.

"I can't."

"Son of a bitch," Foster yelled, punching the air repeatedly. "Son-of-a-goddamn-bitch."

He rushed across the space between them and stood before Poet, squaring his shoulders, inflating his chest. Poet maintained his grip on the rifle barrel, ready to swing hard if things got out of control.

"What is *wrong* with you?" Foster roared.

Poet could smell the sickly-sweet tang of bubblegum on the other man's breath and right behind it the reek of halitosis. He felt like he was going to vomit, and that was a shot, if he had to take it, he wasn't going to miss.

"Get out of my face…sir."

But Foster would not step aside. He stood his ground, bouncing his shoulders. "*Now* you've got some fight in you. Good. *Good*. That's what we need out here. But this? This isn't over. Sure, I could pick up my rifle and end this right now." Without turning, he jabbed his thumb in the direction of the terrorist along the beach. He shook his head. "But I'm not gonna do that."

"We can't just let him go," Poet said. "He's infected."

Foster stepped back, palms raised. "You're right, Corporal. You're absolutely right." He headed over to his pack, which lay nearby, and took from it his E-tool and a coil of rope. He held them both up for Poet to see. "Which is why we're not letting Johnny-fucking-Jihad go. Oh no. We're going to contain our little problem until *you*—" He turned and began strolling along the beach toward the undead terrorist, leaving a trail of boot prints through the sand and swinging the folding shovel like a batter stepping up to the plate "—grow some fucking balls."

Dark Love

Back to the cave in the foothills of the Jebel Akhdar.

Poet lay on his bedroll beside the fire while Foster stood at the cave mouth, silhouetted against a papaya sunset as he scanned the coastline half a klick away through high-powered binoculars. Firelight licked the limestone walls, creating the illusion that Foster's cave paintings were moving – or coming out of the rock. Using the charred end of a piece of firewood, he had drawn a tableau of stick men, dozens upon dozens, their arms and weapons raised toward a sky that contained no sun, only an oversized child-like outline of a bomb falling, seconds from impact. No expression on the men's faces either, just empty circles of stone. And every night Foster added more to their number, more to the eventual body count.

Poet turned his back on the wall art. He found it uncharacteristically nihilistic for someone who seemed as driven as Foster to want to end the world. But you did not know a man until… You did not know a man, period.

Or a woman, he thought.

His eyes turned to the cave's throat. Beyond the reach of the small fire, it led to a kind of shuddering darkness. At night, with the fire low, the dark pushed its way out, closer to the fire, to them. The air was hot, humid. Sweat ticked on his skin like the soft tread of a cockroach. He fidgeted on the bedroll. His hand itched. And that wall with its faceless faces, its wordless payload… It was a little too much to bear sometimes. Back to the cave felt like just that – back to the cave: a regression. The rejection of time and evolution.

You think too much.

That brought a tiny smile to his face. Then, pulled from the darkness: a memory of Mariela saying those very same words to him; not in some dank cave in Libya but inside a tent on a mountainside in Mexico nearly a decade ago.

He picked up the photograph that lay beside him on the bedroll. Held it between the index finger and thumb of his bandaged hand. The circle of blood looked like a dark hole or an eclipsed sun, their faces suspended over it.

Angela and Susie in a moment captured at Disneyland Paris. Mother and daughter looking at each other, wearing the dumb grins of the ecstatically happy.

He had paid for them to fly over from Galveston for five days and nights, but had not been able to join them because of some altercation and revoked leave. It was bullshit but they bought it. They usually did. And the pictures looked better for it: snapshot selfies with just the two of them looking at each other and only each other. Susie, maybe seven or eight in the photograph, holding onto a Goofy soft toy, Poet's avatar on the trip; in every photograph he was not.

She had met all of her heroes. Mickey, Minnie, Donald, Daisy, Pluto the dog. And Goofy, of course… the one nobody was really sure about.

He ought to have been with them in Paris. Taken an open-top bus tour of the city. Visited the Louvre.

Notre Dame. Walked the Champs-Élysées. To remind him it was still the city of love not terror. Held Angela's hand. Looked her in the eye. To remind him he was a man of the same.

It only happened once, he told himself.

But wasn't that what they all said until the violence spilled over again?

It was the PTSD, he thought.

Bullshit.

He lowered his eyes from the photograph to the bloody circle on the dressing of his hand. A blood moon setting on a sky filled with the faces of his family. Eyes on each other and only each other. He wished they would look his way. *Christ*, he thought. Jealous of the girl who stole Angela's heart. No, not stole; that heart was given gladly, and rightly so. Susie deserved the love of her father too, but what love was there left to give? He could not erase what he had seen: the hanging bodies, heads popped like broken Pez dispensers and gathered beneath the creaking ropes and slow-swinging feet. So, what love was there? Only dark love from a heart shrivelled and cancerous from the things the dead left behind, like notes on a pillow but bleeding and with the eyes missing, not dotted with hearts or kisses but missing – the softest parts always the first to be eaten by the flies. Windows to the soul but a home for maggots. What love was there? Only dark love.

He caught Foster's silhouette out of the corner of his eye as the man took a knee by the cave entrance. Thanks to some trick of the dying light outside he looked less like a man than some hunched creature readying to leap.

"You got kids?" Poet asked. When the crouched beast did not reply, he asked again, louder. "You married, Sergeant? Kids?"

Foster did not turn around but swivelled his head to one side and talked over his shoulder.

"Sure. A wife. Four kids. One adopted."

Poet did not try to hide his incredulity. "Four, huh? Wow."

Laughter filled the cave, rolling off the walls so that it seemed to come from nowhere in particular: maybe from Foster at the mouth of the cave; maybe from the dark throat of the cave itself. Poet hated the acoustics of this place. The cave, the world, laughing at him.

"Hard to believe huh?" Foster said. "Guy like me could have himself a family. Well, my secret's out. Now you know where my sunny disposition comes from. How about you? Any kids of your own? A wife?"

"Angela. We've been engaged ten years. One daughter. Susie. Eight years old. Beautiful. Everything we're not."

"You ought to put a real ring on that finger, man, not some placeholder."

"Yeah. I know."

"Iraq was another long engagement, and you know how *that* shit turned out."

Poet allowed himself another smile.

"How long you been married, sir?"

"Seventeen years, November fourteenth."

"Do you miss her?"

"Shit yeah. Been away more than half those seventeen. Feels like I've done more tours than the fucking Stones."

"I know what you mean."

"This may be the last, though."

Poet, still holding the photograph, sat up beside the fire.

"That doesn't sound like you, sir."

"I blindly follow orders, Poet, but that doesn't mean I can't see. This thing is nearly over. It's the end of days, the reckoning, whatever. Things are counting down. We've had three infected in two days. A week ago it was more than a dozen. Week before that, I lost count. One of them must have got off those islands by now, and all it takes is one. A million people, small point of origin surrounded by water, granted, but the potential to spread in any direction. Statistically, there's a chance. We've got trip wires and sensors all up and down the beaches. We've got feet on the ground patrolling the European coastline, boats patrolling the waters, planes in the air, eyes higher up than that, but everybody's got to blink sometime, everybody's got to look away for a second – at something good. We can't all be focussed on this ugly shit all the goddamn time. And what if we all look away at the same moment? Then it's over. I tell you, son, it's the good that kills us in the end. But it isn't the way to live, is it? Thinking about ugliness all the time. It isn't the way to live at all. That girl from yesterday?"

Poet shifted uncomfortably on the bedroll.

"That wasn't your fault. That was on the pilot who pressed the button that dropped your Julius on those poor bastards out there. It's on the OIC who ordered the pilot to press the button, the son-bitch who ordered him, and so on, all the way up the chain of command to the government and God. But both of them enjoy the same perk of the job: zero culpability. For now, at least. Sooner or later, everyone's accountable."

Poet stared as Foster stood from crouching, his silhouette unfolding from a monster back into a man. He joined Poet by the fire.

Poet looked again at the photograph in his hand of his two girls not looking at him, at his wounded palm, a blood moon with a widening corona of pus, and felt the familiar gouge of anguish that came with it. That always came with it.

"In the early days of me and Angela," he said, choosing his words as carefully as he might choose where next to place his foot on an untried roadside. *But wrong words and IEDs sometimes only take the legs*, he thought. Not saying the words, not hearing the words said – that kills you every time. "I spent a few months down in Mexico," he continued. "There… there was this girl…"

Poet laid the photograph of Angela and Susie face down on the bedroll, took a deep breath, and began to tell his story.

I Would Never Be Nineteen Again

Her name was Mariela Peña. But that comes later. Me and some buddies had decided to load up a truck with beer and take a road trip to Mexico. We had money for booze, gas and girls. I wasn't all that interested in the girls because I had Angela back home, but I had to maintain a front for my buddies. Angela and I were high school sweethearts. She was my first kiss, my first everything. But me and my buddies had played high school football together (Go Tors!) and I knew they would not stand for me acting pussy whipped. Someone had forgotten to tell us high school was over. Besides, I was nineteen years old. I would never be nineteen again.

Without anyone coming out and saying it, we all knew it was to be our last walk through the tornado. We all had jobs of one kind or another, and those who didn't had rich folks who didn't mind that their son could not get his shit together. And then there was me. Absent father, crazy mother. Two bedrooms but one missed payment from the trailer park.

Angela was waitressing and I was picking up shifts on construction sites where and when I could, hoping something would stick. What I really wanted to be was a writer, like Bukowski out of Los Angeles. Time magazine had called him 'a laureate of American lowlife.' Time magazine. What that said to me was that you could start with nothing and turn it into something. But Angela was four months pregnant, and that bump was like a tumour on my brain, pressing on a nerve. Try writing even your *name* with a tumour.

Angela kept a tip jar in our kitchen. She was always saving for something, but more often than not she never got it before something else got in the way: life, usually, with its greedy, grabbing hands. She had at least three hundred dollars in singles and change in a mason jar, and I was light for our road trip. So, I borrowed half and left her one of those I-O-U notes on the countertop. She would find it at the end of her shift, and she'd be mad as hell, but she would understand. Angela was good that way. And yet, before we were a half-mile down the I-45, I felt the fires burning behind us. Instead of turning back though, we floored it. That's the difference between boys and men. Boys keep chasing the carrot because they don't know what it is; men know, and they know it ain't worth chasing. One hundred miles and countless Budweisers later, never mind the jay we took to passing round, none of it mattered anymore. I would never be nineteen again.

I don't remember a lot about the trip itself. Small wonder: I was loaded. Thinking back, I wish we had just carried on driving until our money was used up. I liked the road, and the road liked me. When I was a boy, Pops used to take me out for long drives in the middle of the night. He never gave me much, but he gave me that. I remember the sound of the tyres tearing through the dirt. The smell of his cigarettes lingering in the cab. And Toby Keith on the radio, singing *Should've Been a Cowboy*.

When my father left, he took the truck and all our late-night drives with him. He left me alone in that house with my lunatic mother, and though I loved that woman it was a house of tears for the longest time. I came to miss the road at night something awful. The way it never quit but kept on, even with the dark pressing hard against it, hemming it in on all sides. It kept on. But a ten-year-old boy can't take to the road on his own; he needs a man to hold the wheel for him. But Pops could go fuck himself with a bundle of rebar as far as I was concerned. Should've Been a Cowboy? Should've Been a Father first.

I don't recall much of Monterrey or any of the other places we visited during our first couple of days in Mexico, at least nothing that doesn't involve drinking in bars. Me and my buddies weren't into sightseeing much beyond looking at the humps on the beautiful, brown-skinned girls, so mostly we drove around until somebody got thirsty, and then we'd stop somewhere and drink. If I recall, we were thirsty a lot. After Monterrey, we decided to head toward the coast, where we found ourselves on the outskirts of Tampico, in a small strip bar called *La Señoras Locas*. That's where I met Mariela.

It was nothing but a dirty hole in God's green Earth but the beer was cheap and on tap. There was a long oval island in the centre of the floor for the serving girls to shake their asses on between rounds, and a main stage tiled in black and white like a chessboard, you know, for the performance art. At one side of the stage there was a bunch of sex toys set out on display on what looked like a giant shoe rack. Everything from cuffs to love eggs to two-foot double headers. The girls went onstage and sometimes the crowd hollered out their prop of choice. Nothing sexy about it. Nothing hygienic either. It was desperate, like the staring neon everywhere: from dancing girls (as though there weren't enough of them in the bar already) to the words FUCK lit up in healthy vulvic pink and LOVE in a shade of red that coupled with the smell made you think of menstruation. Most of the girls weren't career strippers or professionals either. They didn't tease or intimidate you like they did back home. They were young, inexperienced, demeaned, stumbling on tall heels, waving dildos in the air like flags and they were at Fenway Park, with tanned skin mottled by more than just the occasional bruise, which they did their best to hide with powders or creams that didn't quite match the natural colour of their skin. Between that, the low-level lighting, and what I'd call their strategic dressing, they managed to hide a multitude of things. Even missing toes.

By the time Mariela took to the stage, I was, not to put too fine a point on it, shit-faced. It sounds like I'm making an excuse, and maybe I am, but that's not how I want it to sound. Sometimes words cannot do a story justice, which is maybe why I don't write anymore. Words fail me. It was just something that happened. That's all any of this is, something that happened and not some long excuse, no matter how it might sound. I mean, I can say the words "I would never be nineteen again" as many times as I want, but they're only words, smoke, and my fingers pass straight through them every time. I know what I did. I'm drowning in it. But you can't blame a man who reaches for something to keep himself afloat. Right?

When Mariela walked onstage there was no fanfare. She simply tottered out onto the chessboard wearing black and red underwear, stockings, and skyscraper heels, accompanied by that odd bird-flute intro to *The Question of U* by Prince. The rest of the girls, when they went out, it was like bullets fired from a gun – *boom* and there they were, spreading cheeks in your face or leaning back against the pole, making an inverted V with their fingers, pulling their underwear so tight you got the camel toe or even the vein of their tampon string. It was the least erotic thing I had ever seen, and for them I imagine it was the female equivalent of jerking off when you can't get wood, nothing popping except the sweat on your brow, and that moment, that oh-so-goddamn-wonderful moment, when you look down at this soft pathetic thing sitting in your palm – or in their case, the guys watching them not getting off – this useless lump of flesh and no bone, and you wonder *what the fuck am I doing flogging this dead thing?* But you keep at it until you get that last little drop of self-hatred and self-respect out of you.

Not Mariela.

She went out there and danced liked she was actually listening to the music. Swaying *to* the rhythm instead of thrusting against it. Eyes closed and a smile on her lips. The other girls before her never did that; they scanned the faces of the men in the crowd until they found their mark, smelling out the fattest bankrolls and sticking their pinched nipples in its face until it started ejaculating dollars onto the stage. Mariela kept her eyes closed for almost the entire song, riding the music like she was surfing some beautiful wave of sound. This was around 2007, and somehow she was able to make Prince seem relevant again. Don't get me wrong, she wasn't the best dancer. She kept losing her balance and stumbling. But she had this way of working it into her routine so that it looked deliberate. No tits shoved in your face so close you could see the bite marks; no fake smile. She smiled, but it wasn't at us, at me; it wasn't at the world outside of her own mind. I liked that. I wanted to climb in there with her.

I waved her over.

She ignored me.

I took a twenty-dollar bill out of my pocket, unrolled it, and tried waving again. It bought me five seconds. She crawled over on her hands and knees, snatched the money before I could get one word out, and crawled across the stage again, gifting me a view of her ass in the process. Her thong underwear had slipped to one side and I could see lips. When she went to stand again, she stumbled. I thought it had to be the shoes. Another bill bought another five seconds. This time I went for it.

"I want to fuck you," I said. "How much to fuck you?"

I would never be nineteen again.

I don't remember if she smiled at me or laughed in my face. I said it again.

"'I want'," she said. "'*I want*.' This, the American idea of romance. Fuck me," she said. "No. Fuck *you*."

"I'm serious. I've got money. Tell me how much it's gonna cost."

She took some time to moisten her lips with her tongue. I watched it work its magic around her mouth. She was driving the price up without needing to say a word. She had all the power, and I had to say something to win even the smallest piece of it back.

"You may just be the worst stripper I have ever seen in my life…and yet…yet I want to fuck your mouth."

My face was hot, burning. I felt dirty. Hell, I *was* dirty. The Dirty Poet. In this foreign land, where nobody knew me, I could be whoever I wanted. "I want to cum on your tongue so that when I go home you'll be spitting the taste of me out for a week."

I know: what the fuck, right?

"Nuh-uh-uh," she said. "I will use the mouthwash," although the way she said it, it sounded like mouth*watch*. "I will use the mouthwatch and you will be home and I will be, how you say, minty fresh, you fucking American asshole."

She got up to leave, or to at least move to some other part of the stage where there wasn't an asshole like me waiting for her. I wanted to wish her good luck with that.

"Wait," I said, waving her back. "Wait. Please. I'm sorry. I'm a little drunk and to tell you the truth I don't know how any of this is supposed to work. What's your name?"

She dropped to a squat in front of me. I thought I saw her left ankle tremble as she tried to hold her balance on those towering heels. She looked me over. The music faded to background noise. Prince faded. And I loved that guy. Testament, if ever it was needed, to the power of a woman to make a man forget his god.

"Mariela," she said.

"Hi, Mariela. My name is Chris. My friends call me Poet."

"Poet, huh? Well, let me be honest with you, Mr Poet: your ways with words stinks." Only it came out *steenks*. I loved that.

"You'll get no argument from me. A dick move is a dick move, and that was a—"

"Dick move," she finished.

"Right. We agree on that."

We bumped fists. Mariela had such tiny, delicate hands. Soft skin. I wanted those hands on me so that I could feel big, like the man I was pretending to be.

"Ask me again," she said. "What will it cost."

"Okay. Mariela – what will it cost to spend a little time with you tonight?"

Why is it that even when you know a thing is wrong, when everything is screaming at you *this is wrong, walk away*, you do it anyway? Why is that? *What* is that?

Mariela leaned closer, her face within a couple of inches of mine. I breathed in her exhale. Carbon dioxide. Too much of that stuff will kill you. True fact.

"Everything," she said. "It will cost you everything."

And it did. Yeah.

True fact.

The Mastication of the Light by Shadow

"That's enough for now," Poet said.

He turned the photograph of Angela and Susie face-up again.

He used to carry a more wallet-friendly picture of the two of them, taken in one of those booths that look like a converted Porta-Potty. Angela's tired eyes, Susie's adoring. Big smiles in a confined space. People never seem closer than when the walls are closing in.

After Mexico, he could never quite believe Susie could love him, never really allow himself to be loved *by* her. He did that thing boys – and men – with longer arms than yours do: place their palm on your forehead and straight-arm you so you cannot reach, so that you stand there swinging wild punches, and nothing, nothing ever connects. Susie had her mother.

A mother was enough.

History repeating itself like a broken wheel.

Besides, after Mexico, his love could only exist through distance, in the space between them. They just could not see it, or understand it. And so he had haunted their lives like some ghost until the outbreak gave him a reason to leave without officially leaving. In some strange way, the Russians had brought him back from the dead too. The world was a crazy place. You love what you don't have and what you can't have you love even more.

He wondered where Angela and Susie were right now and what they were doing. The photograph at Disneyland Paris was taken two years after the Porta-Potty picture, the girls standing in front of the famous fairytale castle. High on the fantasy of life. In the cave, firelight danced on the photograph's glossy surface. Maybe it would be better to let the thing burn. Let the whole world burn.

He looked up at Foster, still sitting at the mouth of the cave, and was startled to see the other man staring back at him. Foster gave a tiny shake of his head.

"Don't let go of that," he said, as though he could read Poet's mind. "*That* is good. Let go of that and all this bullshit will crush you like a tsunami."

Poet quickly pocketed the photograph.

"I'd like to hear the rest of your story," Foster continued. "Hell, it was just getting interesting, son. Tell me you tapped that Mexican ass."

Poet shrugged, and then in what felt like a betrayal, he nodded.

"Then why not skip all this goddamn *preamble* and start with the fucking?"

"Because that isn't the story," Poet said. "Not all of it." He lifted his chin toward the cave mouth and the darkness outside. "What are we going to do about him?"

"Our friend? Johnny Cash, the man in black? He isn't going anywhere. Are you ready?"

Poet looked away and shook his head.

"Then I guess we'll see how well you sleep tonight." Foster looked at him askance. "I hope the rope holds. Knots never were my strong suit. If you feel a tap on your shoulder tonight, it sure as hell won't be me – I'm just saying. Sweet fucking dreams."

"She died," Poet said.

There was a moment of silence but not out of any kind of respect; it was more of a gathering of thoughts or a switching down of gears, the engine of their conversation suddenly high-revving and threatening to stall.

"There was an incident," Poet said. "It happened on a beach just like the one out there."

"Don't take this the wrong way, son, but you're skipping all the good parts. You need to go back to the strip club, to the fucking, to whatever good shit there is left in this story, because it sure doesn't sound like it ends well. But what does, right?"

"I think it's a form of suicide," Poet said.

Foster threw him his best *what-the-fuck?* look. "You've lost me, son. Are you saying your Mexican friend killed herself?"

Poet rose and joined Foster near the cave mouth. The firelight at their backs cast long shadows across the uneven ground outside. White asphodels gathered around their shadows. Pale, hungry ghosts.

"I mean the infected," Poet explained. "The girl from yesterday. All of them. And maybe all of us, too. I think they walk into the sea because they're looking for a place – any place – far from flesh and the temptation to consume it."

Foster laughed; it was a pitiless sound that rolled around the inside of the cave. Its echoes threatened to last forever, that is until the shadows in the cave's throat swallowed them and grew bold from their consumption, seeming to push farther out against the firelight.

"That is a theory, alright," Foster said. "And maybe most of us do need to die before we find a conscience.

But let me run another one by you, see if this sticks. Maybe, just maybe, these things walk into the sea because there's more for them to eat over here than there is over there. Could be that, right? Some simpler explanation? What I'm saying is: don't humanise what isn't human."

Poet turned around to the fire and saw that it was dying from not being fed. Its flames craved wood in the way his story craved its own telling.

But what happened once all the firewood was burned, once you used up all of the words?

Darkness, he supposed. The mastication of the light by shadow.

He walked back to the fire, sat, fed it another piece of driftwood. Fed it another. The flames rose greedily to consume it, and the shadows retreated. For now.

"The fucking came later," he continued.

Goddamn Beautiful,
or Close to It

I drank and watched Mariela perform several routines over the course of the next two hours. Each time she danced, she would end up naked onstage except for her shoes. The shoes never came off. She wouldn't let anyone touch them. Men could twist her tits when she shook them in their face or grab and spread her cheeks when she turned around to pick up her money. But not the shoes. They stayed on. One asshole even requested she sit on his beer bottle for good luck. He had an accent like mine. She did it, too, while I turned away and eyed the door and thought real hard about leaving. My friends were scattered around the bar by then, and I glimpsed their grinning faces every so often in the crowd. We'd even salute or wave like we knew each other. With my back to Mariela, I thought about how women like her walked out onto that bare stage every night in front of the feeding eyes of wolves and snakes and moved their bodies to a soundtrack they probably didn't much like anymore, how they revealed themselves one layer at a time until there was nothing left but skin and flesh, before scooping up their sad reward and stepping silently off the stage and back into the shadows. And it struck me there was more to life in those four minutes than I had ever known. So I turned back and there she was, spotlit, centre stage, naked but for her shoes. I didn't see the tourist with the same accent as mine drink from his now blessed bottle and smack his lips. I saw only Mariela's brown eyes focussed on mine and the hint of a smile, like a secret only we could share.

I held out my hand. No cash, just skin. Her palm met mine. I remember her nails were long and painted speckled duck egg blue and that when she stepped down from the stage she tripped and fell into my arms. Her naked body pressed so precisely against mine it was like a missing part I never knew had been missing until that moment, and the smell of her, the smell of her…goddamn, the smell of her.

"Leave with me," I said. "Let's go somewhere. Do something. Get married."

Mariela laughed; flirtatious and about as real as her nails. I wanted to hear her laugh again, unencumbered by this bar full of watching wolves and snakes, in a room somewhere made for two, squeezed into a bed made for one.

"You are very drunk, America."

There was no denying it.

"They say it clouds your senses, but—" I shook my head. "I say it puts you *in* the clouds and gives you the ability to see clearly from them. Leave with me."

She finally stepped out of my hold, and I worried our dance was over before step one. I looked down at myself and for a moment my body was a lump of clay moulded by her impression, perfect round breasts carved into my chest, my heart squashed and beating double-time between the caverns they'd left behind.

The thing about booze is this: it provides you with insights, moments of perfect clarity, but it also offers up some pretty weird shit too. Knowing what is real and what is an illusion is the hardest part. Booze is a search for truth, and truth – well that's what awaits us all at the end of this rainbow of steaming piss. Who *really* wants to find that? The search is the thing.

"Leave with me," I said again.

Straight armed, she pressed her hands flat against my chest.

"I have two more hours," she said. "Maybe then we get a drink somewhere – *if* you are good and don't look at the other girls. Sí?"

"What other girls?"

"I like you, America," she said.

"I like you too, Mexico."

When she walked away her left leg gave a little at the ankle. She stumbled. I wanted to be her crutch. And so I hung around and watched the various incarnations of Mariela with a growing sense of unease, of her slipping farther and farther away from me as she donned each new outfit only to shed it again like skin. Only, for me, it was the wolves and snakes ripping the clothes from her body with the claws of their currency and the teeth of their eyes. And that asshole with my accent front and centre stage with his long-necked bottle of champagne and his beckoning wave. I remember trying to use his head to smash the bottle, but it refused to break, and then I was lying on my back in the dust of the parking lot, nursing a headache of my own.

The moon hung right in front of me. A pale slice of melon in the sky. I thought of my kid who wasn't quite of this world yet, sitting in a highchair at our breakfast table, taking a small bite out of the moon, maybe pulling one of those faces that kids pull when they taste something they don't like, and I pulled a similar face myself.

A pair of legs appeared beside me. Closed-toe sandals, long skirt of many colours. An ankle tattoo I wasn't quite able to make out before a small hand reached down and offered itself.

I stood on shaky legs, one hand pressed to the back of my skull where it hurt, the other pointing at the moon above our heads.

"That – that up there is a reminder that we don't know shit. It knows all the world's secrets. That's why it's smiling at us half the time. Why it's sometimes laughing, too."

Mariela covered her mouth with her hand. "No," she said. "That would be the people stepping over your sorry ass to get to their trucks."

I glanced around, realised she was right, shrugged, and joined in her laughter.

Then I looked at her and said, "Tell me everything there is to know about you. Give me all your secrets, Mariela. Let's wipe that big dumb smile right off the moon's face."

That first time with Mariela was the best sex I ever had. She told me about her life while we stood in a motel room and I pulled her top over her head. How *Papá* died when she was four-years-old, murdered by the local cartel for some unpaid debt. How they displayed his body in the street as an example to others. How his death forced *Mamá* into stripping and prostitution. How *Mamá* died, too, when Mariela was just fourteen, filming some gangbang scene for an internet porn company. Jacked up on *cocaína* to get herself through the ordeal, she overdosed, slipped into a coma, and likely died several minutes before anybody yelled *cut*.

I stopped and drew away. There I was, on my knees on the bed, kissing her breasts while she too was on her knees and sharing this story, this tragic story. So I asked if she wanted to stop – the talking, the screwing, the *talking* – but she only shook her head, grabbed my hand, and pulled it down between her thighs.

"This is good for me," she said, peppering my mouth with a thousand hungry kisses. "I want to get it out."

And so between the kisses she gave breathless bursts of commentary, spilling out her painful past: how she ended up on the streets at fourteen, an orphan giving handjobs to the drug dealers in exchange for food. How this went on for three years until she landed the stripping gig. The boyfriends. Full of anger at their mothers. How one of them would throw his work keys at her after a long shift, and sometimes he missed and sometimes he didn't. At which point she lay forward on the bed, still wearing her long, multicoloured skirt but naked from the waist up, face turned to one side, hair cascading down her back in coils of long chocolate.

I stepped away from the bed and looked for a moment, just looked. She turned her head to look at me and her hair parted across her back to reveal the pale scars against her dark olive skin. They looked beautiful, like the first stars on an evening sky.

At the edge of the bed, I bent and ran my hands up the backs of her legs and thighs, bunching her long skirt as I went, until finally I arrived at the fleshy rise of her behind and the dark crevasse in-between. Nietzsche was right about that; goddamn, was he right.

She lay there and kept telling me things that blew my mind, though what affected me most wasn't the stories themselves but the matter-of-fact way she told them. It was as if they had no right to be secret. She was damaged, but I was drawn to damaged. Back home and once upon a time, Angela had shared her own horror stories with me about her stepfather's roving eye, and the one time his hands developed a wanderlust of their own. But the strangest thing was: after telling me that story all she did was lie to me – about everything. It was as if by passing that negative energy on to me she somehow grew to resent me for it, like I came to embody every cruel thing the world had ever done to her. Or maybe that's just love, I don't know.

Mariela was a second chance before the first fell apart in my hands. All I knew was I wanted to be inside this woman, to burrow into that mind of hers and see the world as she saw it. I knew that when I climbed into the truck and went back home, it was to that empty savings jar and a woman who was starting to hate me for being a failure at life, and maybe a child who would grow to hate me for the same. I wasn't ready to man up. I was nineteen years old. I wanted to *boy down*. Have fun. Live. Fuck.

Fuck responsibility.

Fuck changing diapers at four a.m. when you can't see straight for the sleep crusting your eyes.

Fuck the end of fucking, and for what? Cuddling on a couch in front of the television while passing some crying newborn back and forth like some fake turd at a party? I wasn't ready for that. I wasn't ready.

Here was this wonder, Mariela Peña of Tampico, Mexico, telling me things because she saw something in me. She trusted me with the truth. And it didn't stop with the death of her parents or the long list of asshole boyfriends; oh no, the good stuff kept on coming, and it was like I was feeding off it, following this trail of broken candy through the woods in the hope of hitting some hidden motherlode. And all the while my hand was cupped over her smooth pussy with Mariela lifting her ass just high enough to rub against my fingers.

And then, goddammit, I had some kind of out-of-body experience. Maybe it was the effects of the tequila we had sunk after leaving the bar, but I thought, not now, not *now*.

I found myself standing in the farthest corner of the room watching what was happening all the way over there on the bed. Except this version of me had a good erection. The real me, the one by the bed with Mariela? No wood at all. She was working on it though, on her hands and knees now on top of the sheets, sucking on my nothing while shaking her ass enchantingly, smiling up at me, smiling, with her lips around my failure.

I looked away...and saw the closed-toe sandals discarded on the floor. Looked...saw Mariela's left foot with its three missing toes.

Two, three, and five.

And then I was back in my own body, and things were starting to happen down there, because in some dumb, naive male part of my brain I saw something broken and believed I could fix it, I could be the one to make it whole again. I'd wanted to save Angela, but when it came to her, want and able were like two cousins who don't really talk. *This* I could do. Here was an empty page with my pen poised above it, while the pages back home were filled with nothing but bad poetry.

"What happened to your foot? Your toes..."

Mariela manoeuvred herself until she sat on the edge of the bed. She looked up into my eyes as she let my cock settle semi-erect on her shoulder like some tame pet. And we stayed like that throughout the rest of the conversation.

"Malaria," she told me. "When I was a child. Necrosis, they said. The surgeon, he tried to operate but he messed up and I had to lose them or die, maybe."

"That's why you stumbled and fell into me in the bar…"

She nodded. "My balance is not good. My memory – my short memory – is not very good too. Sometimes I forget names. Maybe not such a bad thing, ah?"

"Why?"

"Men do not want to fuck me. I mean, they *want* to fuck me but not in the right way. They see the toes are missing and think only about what is not there. With men is always what they don't have. They think I am trying to…deceive them, sí? They get mad. This is ugly but true: anger always ends up in the mouth or in the ass." Mariela saw the guilty blush colouring my face and tried to ease it with a smile. "I will give you some poetry. Some poetry for the Poet. The pussy is love. The mouth, the ass, they are not love. The mouth says horrible things, and the ass, well, you know what comes out of the ass. The pussy is love."

"That's goddamn beautiful," I said. "Or close to it."

She flexed her leg and kicked me on the upper thigh. Bruce Lee himself never moved so fast.

"Don't make fun," she said, but she was smiling. She fell back on the bed. "I am being very serious."

"Me too," I said as I lay down upon the heat of her body. "Now – why don't you give me your love?"

She nodded, and then she did.

Feeding on the Days of Now

In Libya, the fire smouldered as the last of its smoke rose in tendrils to disappear into the cracks in the cave roof. Foster's Maglite leaned against a small rock as darkness pressured the borders of its light. He lay on his bedroll, propped on one elbow, and with his free hand formed crude shadow-puppets on the opposite wall. Giant legs tramped across his tableau of stick figures, crushing their skulls, ending their thoughts.

Poet sat behind him, doused in shadow, his back against the cave wall. He was sweating all over, not from the telling of this part of the tale but at the prospect of Foster's reaction to it. He could not bear to look at the man, to see his judgement of him. In fact, he struggled to understand why he had chosen Foster of all people to listen to his – what? Story? Confession? What was it?

Foster has age and experience, he thought. *Maybe that's why.*

But Poet was reaching and he knew it. Older did not mean wiser, and Foster was a good case in point. His father, whatever highway he drove upon these days, was another.

Poet decided it wasn't about Foster. It was about the girl from yesterday. Fast forward a year from now, ten years, and she would remain just that: the girl from yesterday. And now, because of the girl, the story was spilling out of him, unstoppable as the blood from the hole he had put in her face.

Enough.

He rubbed at the bandage on his hand. Sweat made the wound itch unbearably. There was blood on the bandage too. He stared at it and stared at it as it seemed to stare back at him, a spot, an eye, a pool of red spreading across a sheet of white.

He drew his fingers into a fist. The itch grew worse, but the images vanished. For now.

"So it was never better, huh?" Foster asked.

"Never."

"What a tragedy. Knowing the best sex of your life is behind you. Small wonder you're depressed. That must be like seeing the finale of *Six Feet Under* knowing the final episode of every other show you ever watch will feel like the finale to *Lost*. That's fucking tragic, son."

Poet allowed a small smile from where he sat in the shadows. In the time he had spent with Foster there were moments when he thought that in another time and place they could have been friends rather than antagonists. But then the same could be said of anyone, including their enemies. You drew your cards: sometimes you got a pair; sometimes you didn't.

"I thought we'd be together," he said.

"After one night?" Foster laughed and shook his head. "You really are a horny, romantic fool, aren't you?"

Poet chose to ignore the barb. "I saw her leaving stripping behind and the two of us heading off together, maybe buying a small farm somewhere and raising chickens or something. I don't know, I'm not a farmer. We talked about it. But dreams are only good for filling the holes in conversation and not much else.

It was all bullshit: an end to justify our means. I was like Lenny in that Steinbeck novel. Or Coffey from *The Green Mile*."

"John Coffey... 'Like the drink but spelled different'."

"That's the one. Big JC."

"So, what happened?"

"They killed him. Fried him in the electric chair."

"I meant in *your* story, asshole."

"I know what you meant." *I was stalling*, Poet thought. *Trying to decide whether I can tell you the rest of it or not.* "Mariela died, and I went crawling back to Angela."

"You ever tell her what happened?"

"What's that other line Coffey says?" Poet thought for a moment. "'I tried to take it back, boss. I tried to take it back'. I couldn't tell her. And because of what happened we never got married. I dodge the question any time it comes up. I keep moving, moving, moving, constantly. She gets close, I pull away, change the subject. Come to Libya." Poet laughed, but it sounded cold and mirthless in the heat and humidity of the cave. "I reckon it's something in our DNA, that even when we die we keep moving. She doesn't even bring it up anymore."

Foster stretched himself out on his bedroll, yawned, rubbed his crotch a little *too* long. "Sounds like you need to tell the rest of that story, son. You can't keep running from it. The way I see it? That thing we have tied up out there is your past. That putrid, rotting pile that refuses to quit, reaching for the flesh of your thoughts, gnawing on the bones of your spirit, feeding on the days of now – that is your failure personified, wrapped up in black robes and a mask. You need to destroy it. I say tomorrow night you finish telling your story and then pick up your weapon, walk right out there, and put an end to it. Not tonight. Sleep tonight. But you've got the first watch."

Poet leaned back and felt the cave wall hard against his spine. He looked up and saw the roof loom above him, pressing down. Underneath the bandage, his palm spoke maddening words.

"Foster," he said to the other man's back. "What if the killing never stops?"

Foster sighed. "You want a story, Poet? Here's one. I was a kid in my twenties when the towers fell. Then came the war on terrorism, the Iraq conflict – war was everywhere. Hell, I went looking for it. I went on the internet, Liveleak, places like it, and I watched the unedited footage, the unsanitised truth. Bodies blown apart. Heads stuck on some iron fence in Iraq, all lined up as ordinary folks walked by, just going about their daily business like those things were squirrels sitting in a tree. Picture that fence as white picket and the heads as those of your wife and daughter."

"I think I get it," Poet said.

"If the killing never stops but it prevents that image you have in your mind right now from becoming a reality, I'm for it. The terrorists, the infected – it's us or them. I say it's them."

"Okay, I get it. Get some sleep."

"You know, me and some buddies…we used to throw watermelons at passing trains just to see what a TAC-50 round would do when it smashed through one of their skulls."

"Jesus Christ, Foster, I said I got it."

Foster shrugged. "Pleasant dreams, Corporal. Wake me in four."

Grisly Flowers

He is falling into the cave. *El Sótano de las Golondrinas.* The Cave of the Swallows. He has no helmet torch, no helmet, no clothes, no chute. Walls rush past. Warm air buffets his naked body. A sensation of hollowness in his balls as though he recently had sex. He is falling empty, empty falling. He looks around for Mariela but she is nowhere to be seen as he plummets down through the fading purple light. Tiny flashes of white like paparazzi bulbs appear in the walls surrounding him. *Vencejos*, white-collar swifts, watching from the comfort of their nests. He passes other colours too, colours that float like motes of green dust in the light. These green flecks dart out of his way, and he realises they are also birds, green parakeets or *periquillo quila.* The words in Spanish remind him of Mariela, even as he plunges through them toward the unseen floor with no chute and no means of ever slowing down. Mariela spoke the language beautifully. Whenever she taught him a word in Spanish it was like she was saying it for the first time, creating it just for him.

Wait, he thinks. *Is she alive in this dream?*

It matters little. Hope floats but the truth is denser, and he continues to fall and fall.

Besides, he has the words. He will always have them. She comes alive through them.

Then, farther down, deeper down, where the cave floor awaits, a guttural groan rises on currents of air fetid with the stench of guano and death. Somewhere on the other side of the rising dark, a mass of hungry mouths lifts in unison to meet him as he falls. They don't even move out of the way. He crushes them with his impact, but within moments he can feel them twitching and twisting underneath, turning their own broken necks to eat him from below. Then a horde of the undead pours from the dark to tear him limb from limb.

But it does not end there.

There is no easy escape like waking or death. He is held captive by this nightmare, forced to feel *everything*, every sinew stretched taut and snapped like weak elastic, every bone ripped from its joint and broken open to suck and lap at the marrow inside, and the final humiliation of the rending of his private parts, empty and wet-tipped with ejaculate, consumed by hungry, wrenching bites.

El Sótano de las Golondrinas, Mariela says.

The Cave of the Swallows.

Poet woke sweating on the floor of another cave, this one in sight of a long beach in northern Libya. His muscles ached, some of them locked with cramp-like pain, but at least he was…intact. The cramps were a familiar echo of his nightmare, and he knew that in time they would ease enough to allow him to stand and walk off the rest of the discomfort. But there was something new here.

Lying on his side, the floor a vertical wall to his left, he saw silhouetted against the morning light straining to reach inside the cave a pair of silhouettes jutting perpendicular to the floor, the wall.

…*the hell?* he thought.

Disoriented, he used one hand to prop himself into a sitting position and the other to rub the sleep from his eyes. When he opened them again, it was to a pair of legs that ended halfway to the knee, and two brown-skinned hands planted in the torn flesh of either one like grisly flowers, broken fingers splayed in a kind of macabre greeting.

Poet screamed in horror and scrambled backwards across the cave floor. The air filled with plumes of limestone dust.

"Relax," Foster said from somewhere near the mouth of the cave. "They won't bite."

Poet could not take his eyes off the sculpture of body parts. How long had they sat there, mere inches from where he slept?

"You sick fuck." He scanned the shadows inside the cave for Foster but could not find him. "Why – why would you do that? You said you'd leave him… Jesus!"

"I told you. I'm no good at tying knots. The rope didn't hold and that thing worked itself loose. It was headed up here, towards the cave. Must have been drawn to the light. Lucky I spotted it, otherwise it would have been chowing down on you in your sleep."

He *was*, Poet thought, and shivered.

"You're welcome," Foster said.

"Fuck you."

Foster stepped out of the shadows near the cave mouth into the sunlight edging its way inside. Poet could make out his boots and the lower half of his legs, but the light only reached so far up his body, as though the darkness was reluctant to give him back.

"When you think about it, it's how the whole thing started," Foster said.

"What?"

"Life. The human race. All of it. It started with fish dragging themselves across some beach somewhere millions of years ago. Those fish grew legs, and the rest, as they say, is history." Foster lit a cigarette, took a long pull, exhaled a cloud. "Pardon the pun, but we can't let these motherfuckers grow legs. They can't be allowed to evolve."

Poet climbed to his feet and brushed the dust off himself, all the while shaking his head in disbelief.

"Where's the rest of him?"

"Outside. Tied up like some sick old dog. You ought to do the decent thing."

"Why couldn't you finish him off yourself?"

Poet thought he saw Foster shrug. "Maybe I've got a case of what you got," Foster said. "Maybe I'm starting to feel sorry for these things. Maybe I figure we should let them walk out of the sea and take over the world. I mean, it's only us – the living – they want to end, right? So maybe we should let them win, and when we're gone and they have nothing better to do they'll just wander around looking for something they lost and won't ever find again. Just like you, huh, Poet? Fucking pussy."

"Fuck you."

"The Bible got it right," Foster went on. "The meek shall inherit this earth. With nothing else to keep them occupied they'll become pretty meek, don't you think? Without something to fight against, prey on, or fuck over, who *isn't* going to lose the will or the capacity to live? But hey, maybe the world is overdue this change. Sure, it might stink of bad meat and old shit, but so what? Compared to what we've done to it this might be a kindness to old Mother. Maybe what we've got right here—" he grinned and opened his hands towards the grim display of amputated feet and hands "—is the future."

Poet knew Foster was trying to bait him. He also knew Foster was high, though not from any actual drugs, more from the thrill of inflicting violence on the undead terrorist. They lived and operated in a state of abject monotony out here, a flatline existence, and anything that made the line spike was alluring. It was in Foster's tone and verbosity. Unmistakeable, and all too familiar.

Following Poet's return from Mexico and Susie's birth, Angela's suspicions had dragged her into a pit of depression, and how she chose to climb out of that was to turn to amphetamines. He remembered coming home from one failed job interview after another and her launching into these crazed but good-natured rants, in which she gleefully called him a loser and an asshole and accused him of sleeping around. This wasn't all that different. And though he would never admit it to Foster, *his* pulse was racing too.

Poet left Foster alone with his vision of the end of humanity and exited the cave, noting the man's significantly dilated pupils as he passed. He stood under the morning sun, the Jebel Akhdar at his back, looking out over the meadow of asphodel toward the beach and the sapphire-blue waters of the Mediterranean – and then nearly passed out from a rip current of nausea. He suddenly felt hemmed in, trapped. The flowers smelled of nothing, the sea air smelled of nothing, but the wound on his hand…the wound reeked of old blood and sepsis. There was no escaping the stench; he carried it with him wherever he went.

Foster joined him outside. He glanced at the white sea of asphodel in the light of day and recalled walking through it in the early hours of that morning, pallid ghosts floating in the fading dark, parting like smoke around his trudging boots. He was relieved to see they were merely flowers again. But he also saw the path he had forged through them, a trail of blood-stained petals and broken necks. He looked away again quickly. Several white board signs stood aslant around the edge of the meadow, bearing warnings in Arabic. The text looked like finger-smears of blood, deep-red paint, although considering the nature of their warning blood might have been more appropriate. He had not heeded their message earlier after removing their captive's hands and feet; in fact, in his dark reverie he had not seen them at all or chosen his usual path from the beach. He stared at the leaning signs, the Arabic text, and felt a sickness uncoil in his gut. He had carried his grim, dripping payload directly through an old minefield.

Needs must when the Devil drives, he thought. A favourite proverb of his, one that usually gave him strength, so why, he wondered, was he shaking like a dog shitting razor blades?

Adrenaline, he thought.

Sympathetic nervous system, he thought.

Bullshit, he thought.

It was the girls. His daughters. If something happened to him then they were on their own. Carol was out of the picture now, and her parents, the girls' grandparents, they could do little to protect them from what was coming when the infection spread.

No, he thought. They were on their own *right now*.

He thought of his eldest, Katherine, and how at eighteen she had taken on the mantle of parent that Carol had so readily relinquished, doing so without a word of hesitation or complaint. Even while her friends abandoned her for parties and boys, Katherine stayed home and made sure her sisters were taken care of. Carol's parents were too old, too heartsick, little more than names on a document of guardianship. They had been hollowed out by what had happened to their only daughter, just as he had been. The bitterest pill: not to be swallowed but choked on for the rest of your days. Katherine was tough, though; Katherine was young. Life had dealt her the worst cards, but with some hard choices and harder sacrifices, it was possible to change a bad hand to a winning one. Katherine had taught him that, and so she would understand why he was in Libya doing what he was doing. This was no different.

This was no different.

Needs must when the Devil drives. Right?

Both men stared hard at the mirror of the sea. Neither spoke for a while, mindful of the implicit threat of violence that crackled between them like an electrical storm.

From beyond the asphodel meadow, the sound of a thing in pain rose up the hillside. It was eerie: rhythmic but without any sense of panic or urgency; cold pain, *dead* pain, the memory of it rather than the reality.

Poet listened for a moment and wondered if that was what Julius did to you: stripped you of life – the present – and trapped you in the imprinted past, so that all you had access to were the fading memories in your brain, themselves being slowly eaten away by ravenous microbes. He shuddered.

Foster listened to the sound and pictured his daughter Katherine standing at the end of the hallway in her grandparents' home in Philadelphia, shielding her three sisters from the shuffling advance of Carol's folks, and maybe even Carol herself, already something of an expert in the killing of a child. He shuddered too.

Foster spoke first.

"You think you're better than me."

When Poet did not answer, or did not answer quickly enough, Foster continued, "you think because you've found a conscience in all of this that somehow you're better. But you have no right to judge me, son."

"You're wrong," Poet said. "Those hands and feet you left back inside the cave give me the right. You need to get them out of there – *sir*."

Foster clenched and unclenched his jaw. "Maybe they'll walk out on their own."

"What?"

"About a half-hour ago I saw one of them move. While you were asleep. It twitched. Left foot, I think, although if you look closely you'll notice I stood them the wrong way round: left on the right, right on the left, both feet turned out. I used to do that trying to put on my shoes in kindergarten. I was such a dumb fucking kid."

Both men watched as a southerly breeze from the Mediterranean pushed across the asphodel meadow toward them. It brought to their noses the unmistakeable smell of rotting flesh from the vicinity of the beach.

"Now you're a dumb fucking adult, sir," Poet said.

A pause, and then both men laughed. Short-lived though it was, it eased the tension.

"I was making a point," Foster said.

Poet turned to look at him for the first time since leaving the cave. "And what point was that? That you've gone Colonel Kurtz out here? Because I got that point; I got that loud and clear."

"You've heard of Newton's Laws, right? Third Law states that for every action, there is an equal and opposite reaction. Same applies to inaction. What you saw there was my equal and opposite."

"That does not look like inaction to me."

"The son-bitch is still moving, isn't he?"

Poet felt the return of that strong desire to punch Foster squarely in the mouth. He turned away once more. Looked at the Med. *But for the movement of the tides, the world could already be dead*, he thought. The tidal motions nothing more than the twitching of the corpse. Bodily fluids settling into their final torpor.

"Mariela kept forgetting my name," he said, "because of her bad memory. It frustrated the hell out of me at first, but then I kinda made it my mission to leave an impression on her, one so deep she could never forget me. Sad thing is – I'm starting to forget *her*. I can't remember her face like I used to. I remember the missing toes, and I can even remember which toes were missing – two, three, and five. But her face…it's not so clear anymore. Why do you think that is?"

"Beauty fades," Foster said. "Ugliness lasts forever." He held up a hand. "Before you go off all half-cocked on me, think about it. It's easier to remember somebody's imperfections, especially when that somebody has caused you a lot of pain, as this Mariela clearly has." *And Carol*, he thought. *Don't forget what* she *did.* "But it's the things that take that little bit more effort to remember that reveal the most, the *best* about a person. Ever panned for gold, son?"

"Once, with my dad. In Seguin, Texas."

"Then you should know this: the pan doesn't come back with gold every time you put it in the river."

Poet nodded. "Talking about her sure does bring her back."

That's why some of us don't *talk*, Foster thought. *We don't want it coming back.*

"And you'll finish that story of yours," he said. "I promise. But later. First, we've got some work to do on that beach."

After breakfast, which they ate outside the cave, they gathered their rifles and gear and followed the winding dirt path that led to the beach. On the way, they passed several of the white board signs erected around the edge of the meadow. Foster felt nausea rise in his throat and averted his eyes and mind from the dangers that lay buried beneath the roots of the flowers.

Katherine was in college now. Boyer College of Music and Dance, Philadelphia. A vocal arts degree. He ought to be proud, and he was, but the aftershock of Julius turned everything upside down and inside out. What would college matter one month from now if one of the infected made it through the blockade? Better she picks up a gun, a sword, anything but a pen or a fucking microphone.

He wished he had access to a phone. He wanted to talk to her, warn her, tell her where to take her sisters to wait things out. The lodge. He hoped she remembered it. Most of all, though, he wanted to hear her voice again. But they had been ordered to relinquish their phones before their deployment in Libya to keep the story from the world's media. Malta and Gozo were experiencing their 'worst storms in a century' (a white lie really, he thought. It *was* a shitstorm of biblical proportions) and all incoming and outgoing flights were suspended indefinitely. But such efforts at containment were like trying to stop the wind with your hand. Wherever you pushed, the story spilled out somewhere else. Rumour had it that it had become something of a rite-of-passage for young soldiers to bag themselves a selfie with one of the infected. Arm around shoulders, strike a pose, smile for the camera. There was even a dedicated Facebook page and Twitter account. All Foster wanted was a phone call or a few minutes on WhatsApp with his daughters.

Poet and Foster found what was left of the undead terrorist blocking the path to the beach, a rope around his neck, spun several times around a large rock and tied in a tumour of multiple knots. He lay on his front among the rocks and sand. At each of the four amputation sites, there was a pool of coagulated blood and gristle where the cutting had taken place, and where he had spent the entire morning attempting to crawl but finding no purchase. Sand and small stones stuck to the soft parts of his further eroded stumps. Up close, the stench tortured the senses.

Poet recalled Foster's claim earlier that the undead terrorist had been heading toward their cave and realised it was not just a slight exaggeration but an outright lie. He wondered if he had even broken free as Foster had claimed or if that was a fabrication too. Nevertheless, if he had made it off the beach and into the more heavily forested areas of the Jebel Akhdar they would have lost him, and the next communication from command – if any – would be to report an outbreak in one of the towns south of their position. Maybe that had already happened. The radio silence of late could mean nothing, but it could also indicate that the dam was already broken and the flood underway.

"Mind how you go," Foster said. "Ringo here might not be able to play the drums anymore but he can still bite your leg."

They spent the next hour checking the tripwires and dusting the sand off the motion sensors positioned above the tideline. The temperature rose with the sun as the Mediterranean Sea lapped coolly against the shore. Foster's thoughts kept returning to his inadvertent stroll through the minefield earlier that morning. He seemed unable to distract himself from it for very long, but his nausea had given way to intensifying feelings of relief and hope. Luck had clearly been on his side, and luck like that could save the whole goddamn world. At zero nine hundred hours, with the temperature nudging seventy-eight, he stopped work and turned to Poet.

"You know what? Screw it. It's hot, the water's beautiful – I'm going for a swim."

Poet opened his mouth to argue but realised there was little point and so closed it again. Instead, he removed the bandage from his hand and washed the wound in the shallows while Foster stripped out of his gear. A minute later, Foster strode into the blue waters as naked as the day he came into the world.

Poet found a rock and sat, rifle nearby, watching the middle distance for any sign of activity in the sea. In the past, the infected had floated in on their backs, their bellies, and even walked along the seabed.

He supposed their buoyancy depended a lot on the amount of trapped air and gas inside their rotting bodies, and maybe the type and weight of clothing they had on. The Mediterranean delivered them onto the beach in all kinds of varied and arbitrary ways. Even so, the water looked cool and inviting from the rising heat of the beach. He mopped his brow and watched Foster enjoying his swim. But it was impossible to not compare the waters of the Mediterranean to the asphodel meadow they passed on the hillside on their way to the shore. Beneath the flowers there were landmines. Beneath the waves there were teeth.

Earlier, outside the cave, he had noticed Foster shaking and seen the trampled path through the meadow. Dumb luck had saved Foster from those mines. Fast forward a few hours and this was only slightly different: more of a conscious rolling of the dice, but a dice roll all the same. Taking control inasmuch as Foster could. Poet wondered if he would keep rolling though, perhaps take bigger risks, testing his luck until he convinced himself it was actually something else: fate, maybe. A shiver climbed Poet's spine. And what then? Such conviction to reach the next level of stupid was deeply worrying. His story remained untold; Mariela, still alive at the current point in its telling. But a story once started had to end, otherwise it was nothing, a bunch of words with no meaning, a corpse with no final place to rest; and Mariela, she had to be brought back to life, yes, but she also had to die again for the circle to be complete. Who would he tell the story to if something happened to Foster? Someone else? Yes, probably he would, assuming there was anyone left to tell, but even so, there would always be that great unfinished, and he loathed that. Sentences had to have periods. Stories had to end.

Poet stood from the rock, lifted his rifle, shouldered it, peered through the scope. He tracked the trail of splashes until Foster filled the scope's field, scooping water, face blinking into view as he came up for air. Poet's finger found the trigger just as the wound on his palm flared from curling his hand around the grip. The shot went high, higher than he anticipated, and was swallowed by the Med. Through the scope, he saw Foster no longer swimming but treading water, glaring back, no doubt assessing the present danger. Poet lowered his rifle and waved him in to shore.

Within moments, Foster stood naked in front of him. Fear did unflattering things to the man's cock and balls.

Poet grinned.

"What the fuck was that?" Foster's fists were clenched at his sides and struggling to remain there. "What the hell are you grinning at?"

Poet's smile turned into a grimace as he dropped his rifle to the ground and flexed the fingers of his bandaged hand. The pain reverberated up through his arm into his shoulder and neck.

"Well, asshole?"

Poet looked up from his hand at Foster. "I thought I saw something in the water, sir."

Foster spun around to scan the sea, turning his back on Poet. He saw nothing but clear water for half a mile.

If you were trying to wax me, he thought, *then here's your opening*. Point blank, back of the head. Textbook.

"Did you get it?"

"I'm not sure," Poet said. "The shot went high on account of my hand. But I can't see him out there now, so… I don't know, maybe it was a trick of the light. Still, might be a good idea to stay out of the water – you know, as a precaution."

Foster nodded. "Yeah. It might be that." He returned to his gear and started dressing slowly. "Why don't you take a walk? We need some firewood for tonight. While you're on the mountain, take a look around. Make sure nothing slipped by us during the night. I got this."

Poet did not move right away.

"Corporal, thirty seconds ago you came *this* close to turning my head into a canoe, so let me be clear on this: get the fuck out of here. I want to be left alone."

Poet turned and headed back up the beach. After only a short distance, Foster stopped him.

"Hey, asshole!" He pointed down at Poet's rifle, which lay on the beach between his feet. Water dripped from his genitals onto the stock. "Full battle rattle. Who knows what you'll find in those trees. And keep the old brain bucket on too. You never know when some asshole is going to try and take a shot."

El Sótano de Las Golondrinas

Poet stood in a narrow gorge in the upper foothills of the Jebel Akhdar. Limestone cliffs rose above him on either side, dotted with grass and shrubs and the nests of unfamiliar birds. More shrubs festooned the feet of the cliffs, hemming Poet in. An old juniper tree dominated the widest part of the floor, growing near a shallow pool of russet-coloured water, its trunk gnarled and twisted by time and an enduring need to live. Other trees grew in the gorge but they were small, feeble-looking things so parched they might crumble into dust from the lightest touch. Poet looked at these and then at the strong, thriving juniper and thought about how so much depended upon where you made your stand. Fortunate, and the sun would kiss your face; less fortunate, and you cracked and died in the shadows.

Poet had made *his* stand eleven-and-a-half thousand kilometres away, in the Mexican state of San Luis Potosí, in a place called the Cave of the Swallows. On his way to the gorge, he had recalled the hike to the cave. Mariela and he had joined a group of tourists and thrill-seekers, but it might as well have been just the two of them. It had been early evening, not quite eighteen hundred hours, and he recalled the sun slipping toward the green rainforest-covered mountain. They had argued on the path through the trees. Their first argument. A conversation that had started innocently enough but something he'd said had lit the touch paper.

"You're in love with him."

Yeah, that was it.

At that time, it was a blind guess. Despite Mariela's openness and honesty about so many things, there were some doors she would not open. Not yet. Miguel was one of them. Miguel was the owner of *La Señoras Locas*, and Poet suspected Mariela of holding strong feelings for him in the past. He thought that maybe Miguel had rejected her ("You have such a beautiful face, *florecita*, but such ugly feet. I feel I would come to hate your face as much as I loathe your feet."), and he *knew* Mariela owed Miguel some money. She had mentioned a debt often in the same breath as his name. But Poet had suspected – and to the same extent, *hoped* – her feelings for that human monster truck were no more than a devious means to a debt-free end.

"That's it, isn't it?" he said. "He's infatuated with you and you're just playing him?"

On the mountainside, the sun was slipping behind the trees. The distant canopy looked like it could be on fire. Birds chirped everywhere, a cacophony of unseen things talking incessantly with tiny, paranoid voices.

"Take your big words and your big dick and go home, America. Go! Be with your woman and your baby on the way. Fix that little mess before you try to fix mine, sí?"

His name was America. Not Poet, not Chris – because even after a week she still struggled to remember it – but America. And when she was pissed at him she called him nothing else.

"I can help," he said, and in a gesture of intent, he gently held her elbow and tried to steady her on the path up the mountain. The twenty-minute hike to *El Sótano de las Golondrinas* from the road was not an easy one, and Mariela's limp had become increasingly pronounced.

"What are you doing?" she said, and yanked her elbow from the cup of his palm. "I can do this on my own."

He raised his hands in surrender. "Fine, I just thought—"

"You *don't* think, America. That is your problem. You just do something and then, then comes the thinking."

"What are you talking about? I was trying to *help* you. The walk is difficult. The air is thin. We're carrying packs on our backs and climbing a goddamn mountain! I was being nice, okay?"

Mariela looked at Poet askance but with a smile forming on her lips. "You talk like you never climb a mountain before. Stop complaining and try to keep up. *Vámanos.*"

She poked out her tongue and quickened her pace, leaving him behind to move through the others and join the guide out front. Poet stopped for a moment to catch his breath. It wasn't the climb. Back in Galveston, he played football, he ran track. It was Mariela. She was a different kind of mountain. The climb to the Cave of the Swallows was so he could throw himself into a thousand-foot hole. Twelve seconds of freefall with the hope of a soft landing. On Mount Mariela the fall seemed endless, and the landing, if it ever came, anything but soft.

He caught up with her on the approach to the cave mouth. He handed her a cone bearing two generous scoops of melting ice cream.

"The vendor guy promised me this was homemade, although he smiled when he said it. He must really like this stuff though, seeing as he had no front teeth…"

Mariela laughed and accepted the ice cream. As they walked on, she hooked his arm as he was tasting his and brought it round to her mouth. She licked a cool runaway trail from the back of his hand. From the base of his thumb. Her tongue was a beautiful thing. And just like that, they were alone again on the mountain, the name of Miguel melting away like ice cream under a hot sun.

"Chocolate and almond," Mariela said. "With a little touch of cinnamon and – oh yes – spice, of course."

Poet grinned. At that moment, the path began to curve and somewhere up ahead the guide announced, "*El Sótano de las Golondrinas*. We are here, people. And just in time to watch the dance of the swallows."

Nearly a decade later, in a gorge in the foothills of the Jebel Akhdar, the Green Mountains of Libya, Poet took a mouthful of water from his canteen and closed his eyes. He could almost taste the ice cream on his lips, almost feel the tip of Mariela's tongue on the back of his hand. He raised the same hand in front of his face now and saw on the bandage a circle of yellow pus rimmed with blood.

In Mexico, sunset arrived on the mountain, and against the darkening sky the swallows began their evening homecoming ritual. Thousands of white-collared swifts amassed themselves in a vast cloud over the mouth of the pit, swirling and billowing as one. Every so often, a group of ten or twenty birds broke away to dive into the cave, back to their nests. Every so often, the cloud dissolved in a beautiful and delicate explosion, scattering itself like black confetti and then, almost magically, reforming to continue the dance.

Little by little, one by one, the birds came home.

Into this, Mariela threw herself, and moments later Poet followed. Their freefall lasted ten, maybe twelve, seconds, but in those precious seconds they became part of the dance. Mariela's screams of exultation rose to greet his on the warm breath of the cave as he plummeted after her into the darkness. Chasing but never catching. And then her chute opened below him like a spring flower, and seconds later his too, and together they glided slowly down to the cave floor.

A local guide met them there. He wore a white breathing mask to protect his lungs from long exposure to the guano. He spoke Mexican to Mariela for a few moments, while Poet stared and stared up at the spot from which they had just thrown themselves.

"He says we can use the stairs or we can fly. Our choice."

Mariela. Smiling the most beautiful smile. Catching him off-guard.

"Fly?" Poet said. Still feeling the thrill of the fall and the relief of his chute opening, he wanted to reach for her and kiss her, to somehow channel what he felt in that moment and share it. The way she was smiling at him, he could tell she felt the same. But the guide… he stood waiting for his answer.

"Rope," Mariela explained. "Attached to our harness. They will lift us out. But it could take two hours, he says. The winch is powered but very slow. And sometimes it locks."

He recalled the guide telling their group that there were more than five hundred steps down to the cave floor and more than five hundred steps back up. A climb of twenty to thirty minutes. He shrugged. "Screw it, let's fly. I'm not ready to stop."

On two separate lines thirty feet apart, they were winched from the cave floor. Far above, the sky was a circle of crimson flecked with black, as though the world had become fire and ash. Poet felt reluctant to return to it, but his feet were now two storeys from the cave floor and so it was no longer his choice to make. They had leapt off the face of the Earth, and they were returning to it, his problems not left on the floor beneath with the fat insects and the bird shit, as he had hoped, but shed like old skin at the lip of the cave. Leaving the place felt like stepping back into the old. But he knew the fit would never be the same.

He looked to his left and in the dark the light from his helmet torch found Mariela. Even in an orange hardhat and a harness, she could somehow steal his breath away. He opened his mouth to say what was on his mind – and what better place in the world was there to say it, floating through a deep cave, warm air on your skin, swallows and green parakeets flying around you in their thousands, the whole place alive with the sound and activity of birds and yet everything fading, fading to background noise as the walls contracted and the space between you and her seemed to shrink from thirty feet to five to one. And even though the world may be on fire above you, you were rising to meet it, together, attuned to the heat like mercury through a tube. And the reason you saw only fire and saw only the end was because you were mindful of time. How it was running out, its ever-increasing value, and maybe the greatest reminder of them all: how little of it you had left. The rope may snap a moment from now and you have not said the one thing you wanted to say.

But perhaps sensing what he was about to do, Mariela turned to him and spotlit by his gaze gave him a look that said, *Drink…but do not drown*. And then, a sad smile of condolence and the words: "There is nothing else to say."

A little over an hour later they reached the mouth of the cave. As soon as they removed their gear they ducked inside their tent and began kissing on their knees and undressing each other with ravenous urgency. She kept her mouth pressed insistently to his throughout, as though attempting to crush any attempt he made to talk. When he moved to kiss her neck, she moaned and held the back of his head, fingers twisting through his hair, pressing him, holding him to her skin. Then she held one arm under her chest and lifted her breasts toward him. He hungrily accepted, taking one of her nipples in his mouth, running his tongue over and around it. She moaned and, still on her knees, reached for his cock and found it ready, but when he looked into her brown eyes and opened his mouth to say something she squeezed him so tightly the only sound that could escape his lips was a gasp. Frustrated, he spun her around and pushed her forward onto her hands and knees. Using his tongue he readied her then entered her from behind. She gasped and pushed back against him. He grabbed her hair and pulled on it hard enough to evoke a moan but no words. He withdrew as far as he could without slipping from her warmth then pushed hard and fast and all-the-way deep. She cried out in surprise. But no words. And on it went like this for some time, with him trying to fuck the words out of her and her pushing back, swallowing him and everything else with her heat and her silence. And when they came, it was enormous but bereft, a long, shuddering release in which his whole being emptied into hers and hers emptied into his with one passing the other like ships beneath the cloak of a dark and soundless night. He fell onto her as she collapsed under him, pinned, sweating bodies stuck together but not a single word uttered between them, never mind two, never mind three.

Standing in the gorge in the Jebel Akhdar, Poet rinsed his mouth with water from his canteen and spat it on the dry ground near the base of a tiny sapling. The taste of Mariela faded from his lips, but the memories remained. He removed his helmet and poured water over his hair and face. This did not erase the memories either, but its brief cooling effect returned him to the here and now.

Firewood, he thought. *We need firewood.*

There was plenty of it scattered across the floor of the gorge. The bones of all the trees that had perished here were gathered in the long-reaching shadows of the old juniper. Poet imagined the battle waging silently under his feet, beneath the grass and rock, as the long powerful roots of the giant shouldered aside the short reachings of the saplings as they clamoured to drink from the pool or of the moisture soaked into the earth around it. Poet went to the pool and filled his helmet with the brown water then returned and doused some of the shoots that had punched through the hard topsoil into shadow and a hopeless future. He made several trips to the pool and back, until every one of the saplings had drunk well. Then he carried his hand axe to the old juniper and started swinging at its lowest branch, just within reach. When it finally fell away, he dragged it behind him through the dust and sand, out of the gorge and back to the cave.

To the Throat

Foster stood up to his ankles in the Mediterranean and watched the horizon. Where the blue sky met the blue sea there was a kind of unreachable blur. That was where he would put her now. Where he could never hope to find her again.

Fuck you, Carol.

Somewhere out there was the bullet Poet had fired, lying on the seabed, covered by shifting sand, buried at sea. Meanwhile, he stood alone on the shore, water swirling around his feet, angry because Poet took the shot; angry because he missed.

Kate would be so *proud you're feeling this sorry for yourself,* he thought. *After everything that's happened, you don't get to do that.*

At age eighteen she picked up the pieces after Carol got behind the wheel and ruined all of their lives. What did *he* do? He ran. He drank. He fell over. He got up, made calls, pulled strings, dried himself out just enough to pass the medicals, and then he left to guard some lonely stretch of beach against an apocalypse that may or may not have already happened. Meanwhile, back home, his eldest child protected his other daughters from the one that most certainly had.

But this is good for them, he told himself. To have a parent who provides financially but is not around to make any mistakes. It's what every child truly wants. And it's good for him because he can believe he is doing something righteous over here while not having to look in the eyes of his daughters and see their disappointment and hunger for the thing they lost.

They lost their mother.

He lost a wife and a best friend.

He understands Poet's pain only too well. He gets it. Which is why he dislikes the soft son-of-a-bitch so much. He had his shot, he missed, he needed to move on with his life—

There was something in the water.

Well, I'll be, he thought. Maybe the asshole had spoken the truth.

Foster grabbed up his tactical rifle and looked through the scope.

It was a male, naked, the skin on its back severely blistered from a combination of decomp and the heat of the sun on it for however long it had been out there. It looked like a corpse, which was possible, he supposed, as not everything that washed up on their shore then got up and tried to eat them.

In the first twelve hours after Julius dropped, tens of thousands of Maltese, Gozitans, and foreign tourists had tried to flee the contagion. While stationed at the Joint Force Training Centre in Poland he had live-streamed military footage of every kind of vessel from cargo ships to fishing boats piled high with desperate, clinging people leaving the ancient city of Valetta's Grand Harbour. What those people did not know was that the initial symptoms of Julius took anything from twelve to thirty-six hours to manifest. Suddenly every neighbouring port was closed and the captains of fleeing vessels instructed, often at gunpoint, to turn their ships about and maintain a distance of three miles from the European, African and Asian coastlines until such time as someone figured out what the hell was going on. Within hours, the infection took hold and the boats effectively ate themselves. Those not infected and not eaten leapt for their lives into the Mediterranean. Official reports later said there were zero survivors, but it did not take a genius to figure out that even the best swimmers eventually grow tired, and that with nothing to cling to, everyone drowns.

To Foster, it echoed the plight of the millions of people displaced by the bitter feud between Assad and the Syrian rebels, the use of sarin gas in the Ghouta attacks in Damascus, and the Jews three-quarters of a century earlier, forced to flee Nazi dogma or take a shower.

But this time it's a long bath as well as a multinational agreement to look the other way, he thought.

His unidentified floating object was thirty feet from the shore. It showed no sign of movement but Foster walked backwards out of the shallows and raised his rifle anyway.

"Come on," he muttered under his breath. "Get up, you son of a bitch. Get up."

It flitted across Foster's mind for a second time that this could be what Poet had seen in the water earlier. But thirty minutes had passed since then: why was he only seeing it floating out there now? On that basis, he dismissed the idea and stuck to the belief that Poet's shot had been meant for him.

Another two minutes passed before the Med finally spilled the unidentified male onto the shore.

Foster kept his rifle trained on the back of its skull, finger poised on the trigger for any sign of what the politically correct would call PILD: post-infection life disorder. He laughed through his nose at that.

Assholes, he thought.

And then the thing moved.

He chose not to fire, but backed up another few steps instead, giving it some room.

"Identify yourself."

It was trying to stand. Muscle movement after so long in the sea not moving caused the cracks and blisters across its back to split and burst. Dark pus-threaded fluid spilled over its love handles and spattered onto the sand and rocks on the shore. The smell was abhorrent. Foster smothered the lower half of his face with his forearm to try and block it out, but the stench seemed to enter through his pores.

"No third chances. Identify yourself *now*."

It did not answer. Nor did Foster shoot. It was on its hands and knees, head hung low. Wet sand caked its forehead and clung to its hair. He let it rise to its feet, which took it some time.

When it finally stood in front of him, it lifted its head and glared back through one bloodshot eye. The other eye was gone; fish food probably. It was Poet's height, a little over six foot, and Poet's age, late twenties, early thirties, but in the looks department he thought it definitely had Poet beat. He noted that the frontal skin was not nearly as baked as the back, with fewer suppurating sores and blisters, but even so, the saltwater had not been kind. Skin hung on wasted muscle like near-translucent strips of dough, and bones stretched that dough even further in places, not with the threat of pushing through but with the promise. It was a thing at war with itself.

Foster backed another five steps across the beach, reseated the rifle butt in the pocket of his shoulder, and applied a pound of pressure to the trigger.

In front of him, it drew back its cracked, oozing lips and bared its teeth. Then it lifted its arms to around chest height and held them in such a way that it seemed as if it were trying to point its own imaginary weapon back at him.

"Are you copying me, asshole?" Foster said. But he found it pretty amusing. Clearly, there were still some synapses firing inside this thing's brain. "Alright, let's do this. You draw first. How does—"

What it did was give him an idea.

He undid the chinstrap and removed his desert camo helmet.

"Here," he said, holding it out. "Put this on."

The thing reached out and then took an awkward step forward, it's one good eye never shifting focus from Foster's exposed face.

"Let me help you with this."

Foster darted forward and placed the helmet on the thing's head. He did not hang around long enough to fasten the chinstrap as the thing attempted to grab him. After days of inactivity and exposure to the elements the infected were slow and uncoordinated, he knew, but a single misstep resulting in a scratch, a bite, or any breaking of the skin would mean the end. *Or the beginning*, he thought, *if you want to get all existential about it.*

He lowered the rifle long enough to reach down and draw his boot knife. He passed it handle-first into the thing's right hand.

"Let's try something," he said, and stood back to take a long, thoughtful look at the undead islander in front of him. "You know, you really do look like that son of a bitch."

He snapped a salute.

A dozen feet away, the thing raised its right hand to its right temple. The boot knife clinked harmlessly against the rim of the helmet.

"That's good," Foster said. "Now, try this."

He saluted again, but this time he snapped his right hand to his right cheek, just below the eye.

The islander mirrored the motion of Foster's arm and opened its cheek with the knife-blade, water-softened skin splitting like chiffon. Freshets of dark, infected blood coated the right side of its face, running down its neck and onto its chest; from there it dripped and spattered onto the sand.

"Good. Real good. Now, this."

Foster snapped his hand to the corner of his mouth.

"Great smile. Now, this."

Snap to the chin.

"Good, son. *This*."

To the throat.

"Yeah, sweet spot, right there. One more…"

To the throat.

"And again…"

To the throat.

"And again…"

To the throat.

To the throat.

To the throat.

Were There Ever Sunflowers?

Neither man spoke for a while. They sat at opposite ends of the cave and they ate and they listened to the firewood snapping like bones. Over on the cave wall, Foster's tableau of soldiers swayed to the rhythm of the flames. Either they were trying to escape the bomb suspended over their heads or they were worshipping it through some strange ritual dance. It was unclear.

Poet moved his food around on his metal chow plate. Foster's plate sat on the floor, empty, licked clean.

"So you went back to her, eh?"

Poet raised his head, a distant, distracted look on his face. Since that afternoon in the gorge, he had been debating whether or not to continue sharing his story with Foster. But that day at the cave, the jump, the freefall, what happened – or *didn't* happen – in the tent afterwards, it kept replaying over and over in his mind like a movie, shifting in and out of focus. New details emerged as other details faded into frustrating obscurity. His memories were quicksand. Nothing stayed the same. Sharing them helped, the act of transferring the thoughts and images in his head into actual words, releasing them through his mouth, releasing them…yes, it helped.

Okay, he thought. They would stand on the quicksand together. At least that way, if the apocalypse dropped, there was a better chance one of them would survive and the story would live on.

"Sorry, you said something about…"

Foster repeated his question. "I know I'm jumping ahead here but…you said you went back to your wife, you know, after the Mexico thing."

"We weren't married," Poet said. "I mean, we're *not* married – still."

"Of course. I knew that. So, what was it like? Going back. After everything that happened."

Foster had to stop himself from shaking his head. *Smooth*, he thought. *Real smooth. Look at his face. He's thinking, 'Why the fuck does he wanna know that?' And then what are you gonna do?* Tell *him?*

Poet's mind went back to the gorge, to pouring water on the doomed saplings. It had brought a moment of peace for him, a frisson of reality after the cave and the sex and the sex and the cave. For a few moments, he had been back home in Galveston with Angela and Susie, watering sunflowers. 'Because if you're gonna grow flowers you gotta go big, right sugar peach?" Right?

Right?

Did that happen? he thought. *Did I say those words? Stand in that garden? Were there ever sunflowers?*

Easy answer. One word, two letters.

So…why think it if it never happened?

Because I'm drowning, he thought. *She told me not to but I did it anyway. Mariela: she said drink but do not drown, and she was so clear about that, so goddamn adamant, and what did I do, what have I done ever since? I've drowned.*

"I saw smoke earlier," he said, changing the subject. "From the beach."

Foster nodded. "Another tourist. It's taken care of."

"I didn't hear a shot."

"That's right, you didn't."

"What did you do?"

"I took care of it."

"What did you do?"

"What do you think I did? I turned it into a fucking Pez dispenser. Actually, it did that to itself. And quite a show it was, too."

"Why do you try so hard to shock me?" Poet asked. "What's in it for you?"

Foster considered his answer for a moment.

"I don't like surprises, son. Never met one I didn't hate or wish never happened."

"Never?"

"Nope. Not that I can recall. Goes back to what we talked about before, how ugliness sticks in the mind. I say let everyone else have their surprises, but not me. So, tell me – what was it like going back?"

"Why is it so important to you? I haven't told you the rest of the story yet."

Foster broke eye contact for the first time during their conversation. He eyed the exit to the cave. "I want to know if there's ever a way back…"

Will I ever be able to look into the faces of my daughters again, he thought, *and not see Carol looking back at me in every one?*

"It's complicated," Poet said. "And it certainly isn't easy, I can tell you that."

"So the answer's 'no'. There is no way. Just what I thought."

Poet looked at his hand, picked at the edges of the bandage, shrugged. "Truth is – I don't know." He watched as Foster brushed the dust on the floor with his fingertips. "I don't think that's what you wanted me to say, is it? I'm sorry, but it's all I've got."

"Doesn't matter, son. Why don't you go ahead and finish your story."

"I don't think I can do it, sir," Poet said. "The killing. The ending. The…whatever you want to call it. I don't think I can pull the trigger."

"The hell you can't."

"I can't do it because I'm just like them," Poet explained. "The infected, the terrorists, the infected terrorists. I feel dead inside. I walk and I talk and I eat and I kill, and I feel nothing doing it. That girl I shot, that young woman…she reminded me of Mariela, it's true, but it wasn't that, I mean it wasn't *just* that, it was… I felt no remorse taking her down, sir. Nothing at all. Does that make sense? I suppose it does, to you. I mean—"

"Fuck you. You don't know what I feel."

"That came out all wrong. I just—"

"I know what you meant," Foster said. "Anger, son. That's what *I* feel. That's what keeps *me* going. And the moment I stop feeling that anger is the moment I stop feeling anything, and a life without feeling isn't a life at all – right? Is that a good enough answer? Can we move the fuck on now? Tell your story. I'm done talking."

"You can't go back," Poet said.

"What?"

"You wanted to know if there was ever a way back. I'm saying there isn't. It won't work. You'll try, and it will seem like it's working for a while, but you'll be lying to yourself and to each other. It won't work."

Whatever pattern Foster had been drawing in the dust on the floor, he dragged his fingers through it and brushed it away.

"And so here we are," he said, spreading his arms wide apart. "Here we find ourselves. Two sorry fucks in a cave in Libya. And who knows – we may be the last two sorry fucks to walk this Earth. Thank you, son, for your honesty. I already knew the answer. In my heart, I knew it. But sometimes you need to hear someone else say the words you've been thinking all along, right?"

Poet nodded and brushed at his eyes.

He looked at his hand expectantly.

Saw only dust.

Adrianna

Something was different after we returned from the Cave of the Swallows. I knew in my head that this thing with Mariela was going nowhere. My heart and cock didn't know it, but the rest of me – yeah, it knew. We drove the thirty minutes back to our hotel in Aquisimon in silence. It's a rough road and it bounces you around a lot. I was in a strange mood, like I was stood back at the edge of the cave, staring into the black abyss while someone or something was shaking me hard, trying to snap me out of my daze. By the time we arrived at our hotel, I needed a drink. So we dumped our gear in our room and I headed downstairs to the bar while Mariela freshened up.

There had been a mix-up with our booking: twin single beds instead of one double. It hadn't bothered me much when we checked in, but now it was like fate laughing at my expense. I felt like my parents before my father left. I wondered, probably like my father did so many times, whether we'd end up pushing the beds together that night or just lying there in our coffins, dressed in cotton pajamas, reading some book. My father read so many books in his life, let me tell you, it was small wonder he vanished and became something of a fiction himself.

So I sat in the bar and ordered a pitcher of beer and a bean and rice burrito and I looked around at the other patrons. Tourists mostly: sunburnt and tired but smiling. Mariachi music pumped into the bar from hidden speakers. Low volume and too much brass: not so much a taste of Mexico as a junk-food spread for the ear, and about as truly authentic as a red die with the words *Las Vegas* stencilled on it. But I liked my table. It was dark and rustic and covered with old wounds.

The waitress arrived, carrying a tray. She wore a traditional Spanish-style dress and an ear-to-ear smile that could easily land her a job at Disney's Epcot World Showcase.

"I hope the beer tastes better," I said under my breath.

"Pardon, señor?"

I smiled politely and shook my head. "Nothing. Sorry. Please continue."

All the fakery was making me feel a little homesick. At least I understood the fakery back home, most of the time. For all her faults and mine, Angela loved me. She lied about everything else under the sun but not that, not that. Three words and eight hundred miles away in Mexico, I couldn't get a stripper with missing toes to commit to saying it. I felt shitty for thinking of Mariela in those terms, but goddammit I was mad at her. Three missing toes. Three missing words. I was looking for poetry: rhyme and reason in what simply wasn't there.

The waitress dropped a number of paper coasters on my table. Maybe she thought she was working in a casino, dealing cards. Whatever. It rubbed me the wrong way. Here was this table, covered with scratches and marks, the only authentic thing in the place, with probably more stories to tell than the Bible, and she wanted to – what? Save it from a few drops of spilled beer or the bottom of a glass? I wanted to tell her: don't protect it when it wants to drink. When it wants to feel the glass, full, empty, and all the stages in between. It is not sacred. Love is not sacred. We ought to embrace it – each other – like wrestlers, beating it as it beats you. We should not bow to it from a respectable distance and then walk away, or – fuck that – throw paper coasters on it and serve up drinks.

"Are you okay, señor?"

I wanted to pour out all of that stuff filling my head, making me feel nauseated, but I looked around at the tourists in the bar and my Disney Epcot waitress with her emoticon smile, and I gave up, gave in, and said, "Yes. I'm fine. Thank you."

Because the world does not want to know the truth.

"You are staying at the hotel tonight, señor?"

I nodded.

"You are with Adrianna."

It wasn't a question, which threw me for a moment.

"No," I said. "Her name is Mariela."

The smile wavered, returned, but stayed out of her eyes.

She stood a glass on one of the coasters and made ready to pour the beer from the pitcher. I held up a hand to stay her and with the other moved the glass, picked up the coaster, and tossed it like some flimsy Frisbee onto the floor.

"Carry on."

She poured.

"You visit the cave. El Sótano de las Golondrinas."

Again, no inflection, like she was reading from a script she didn't really want to audition for. She finished pouring my drink and stood the pitcher next to my glass on the table, ignoring the other coasters she had dealt earlier.

"We did," I said. "We watched the birds return to the cave at sunset and leave again in the morning at sunrise. It was beautiful."

"Sí. Usted está en peligro."

"What? I don't—"

"Her name is Adrianna. Ask around the club. La Señoras Locas, sí? Ask around. Do not go to the beach."

"The *beach*? What are—"

"She takes them all to the beach. I must go now, señor. I will come back when your burrito is ready."

And just like that she turned and walked away.

Straight into Mariela.

The waitress almost dropped the empty tray, but somehow managed to hold onto it. Mariela reached out and took hold of her above the elbow, below the sleeve. She wrapped her fingers around the waitress' arm and nodded at her once, like they were old friends. When she let go, I saw the ghost of her fingers fading on the woman's arm.

The waitress left our table. She returned just once, with my burrito. But there was something wrong with her smile. A broken connection. She couldn't seem to hold it anymore. It reminded me of a flickering neon sign outside of some hard-to-reach motel. And anyone who has ever seen the movie *Psycho* knows that motels hold some pretty dark secrets. I wanted to apologise to her. I wanted to know her name. Mostly, I wanted to know what she had meant by 'She takes them all to the beach.' But Mariela sat next to me, crossed her legs high under the table, showed me those delicious, thick thighs of hers, and laid a hand over my crotch. She didn't move it; she didn't have to. A little pressure was enough. I managed three bites of my burrito before she led me by the hand back to our room. Housekeeping was in there doing their thing, but she ushered them out. Before the door swung shut she was going down on me.

She begged me to come on her face.

I felt like a god.

But I guess that was where she wanted me, because gods – they don't see a thing until it's too late.

Do You Have Any Secrets?

The next morning we checked out of our hotel and left Aquisimon, taking it in turns to drive Mariela's Nissan clunker back to Tampico and *La Señoras Locas*. Mariela was working that night. I was driving. We were on Federal Highway 70 and making good time. Mariela had her right foot on the dashboard, painting her toes and hitting every red stroke. I decided to turn off the radio.

"I've got nowhere to sleep tonight," I said. "I'm like a hobo now."

I had checked out of my hotel in Tampico before our trip to the Cave of the Swallows. My friends were already back home in Texas. Once I'd met Mariela I had no friends. I figured there would be other road trips, other excuses to get drunk or high or both; they could let me have this one. At least Angela could not call me in my room anymore, demanding to know when I was coming home. *In a few days* was my standard reply, but that only worked for so long, a few days in fact, and a few days became a week became two became three. Now she would be getting worried, but any tears she wept were because I was not there and not because she missed me. There is a subtle difference. What's a puppeteer without their puppet? A sadsack with a bunch of wood and string and nothing much else to do.

"Will you go now?" Mariela asked, practically reading my thoughts. "To your woman?"

"Why – do you want me to leave?"

She did not answer.

I was driving.

"I'd like to stay a little longer," I said. "With you. See how things work out."

"Okay."

I laughed at the show of commitment.

"So can I stay at your place or do I have to sleep in your car?"

"Hmm, that is a difficult choice. Let me see…"

"Bitch."

"Asshole."

I love you.

Nada.

But *I* was driving.

"Mariela?"

"Yes, America?"

"Do you have any secrets?" I was thinking about the waitress back at the hotel bar.

Mariela painted the pinkie toe of her right foot and lowered the foot to the floor. She propped her left foot on the console. I barely gave the missing toes a second glance as my eyes were drawn a little higher to her ankle tattoo: a long feather with its barbs peeling off, turning into tiny birds – swallows. I wasn't sure if it was supposed to draw attention away from the foot or if its message was that something free and beautiful can come from something lost; all I knew was I loved it, and I loved her.

"I have told you a lot of things," she said.

"Yes, you have. But what I'm asking is, is there more?"

She looked up from her nails. Wide smile, bright eyes.

"Of course I have secrets. You know me only a little time. You can't know everything in a few days or weeks or even years. You can't know everything too because then what is there left? Where is the fun then?"

She made a good point. She usually did.

"So basically you're Pi…"

She laughed. "Pie? I *must* hear this…"

"Not pie like the kind you eat. *Pi*, as in the letter of the Greek alphabet, as in the mathematical symbol. Pi. 3.14. You know Pi, right?"

"If you are going to talk mathematics then *I* will drive and you can walk your ass back home."

"I only meant you're complicated," I said. "Deep. There's a lot more to you than 3.14."

She looked at me, and the words were there, right there on her lips: how she felt. Poised and ready to jump.

She painted a toe instead.

"3.1415926536," she said, punctuating every other digit with another flick of the brush. "That is Pi to ten digits after the decimal point, sí? Most people, if they know it, know it only to two, like you. I can go to fifteen if you like…"

I looked at her, open-mouthed.

"Don't tell me you're the Mexican Good Will Hunting or something? How do you know that?"

"Because I do. Because other people don't. And because *Papá* was a teacher at high school before he got involved in the *cocaína*. I will give you one guess what he teach…"

"You played me, didn't you?"

She painted the last toe on her foot.

"Sí." With a nod and a shrug. "How do you like dem apples?"

"Damn, girl. You're—"

"Good? Sí. But what you must understand is secrets don't need to be bad. Secrets can be good too sometimes."

Yeah, right, I was driving.

A Butterfly in Uncertain Metamorphosis

The place had changed. After flying out from the Cave of the Swallows, *La Señoras Locas* felt like rolling in waist-deep guano and crawling bugs. I sat at the bar, away from the solo podiums and the main stage, nursing a watered-down beer. Between performances, the girls walked the floor wearing thongs that didn't quite sit right no matter how much they pulled them out of their ass. There was no symmetry and sweat beaded their cheeks. They talked to men while bending over their tables, like air hostesses on some doomed flight. They wore painted-on smiles to reassure their passengers, but when they thought no one was watching a dead-eyed look sank into their eyes. Instead of a crash, it all ended with strangers spilling on their tits. I bet some of them dreamt of flames. Then I saw one of them walk out from behind a purple curtain, ass like a bruised peach, Kleenexing her face, neck, and chest. She tossed the sodden tissue on the floor and started serving drinks from a tray. The glass in front of me had a clear thumbprint on the rim that wasn't mine. I stopped drinking. Waved over the barmaid.

She was a tall blond, twentyish, pale and thin as a waning moon. She wore daisy dukes and a pink halter. She had a navel piercing that Winked when the light caught it and a sugar skull tattoo low on her hip.

The eye sockets were visible above the shorts but she would have to pull them down a little to show you the teeth. Guys probably asked her about that thing all the time, thinking she put it there because she wanted the attention. The truth probably was it was there to weed out the assholes with no imagination.

"Hi," I said. "I think I need another glass here." I pointed at the thumbprint.

She nodded and returned a minute later with a fresh drink.

"Hey, I would have been happy with a new glass, but thank you."

"No problem," she said, and smiled.

I noticed two things about her: her accent was American and they made her wear too much makeup. *No one* wore that much makeup through choice. I wondered if she applied it with a tar brush. It was like funeral makeup, except corpses tended not to smile or move their faces around much. Not then. It creeped me out.

"New here?" I asked.

"Couple of weeks. Just passing through. Need the extra money. You know how it is."

"Yeah, I do. I thought you might be – new, I mean. You look like you've got one foot in this place and the other still outside the door."

She laughed politely. "Yeah, kinda, I guess."

We made small talk in-between her serving drinks. Her name was Ashley. She went to Texas State. Her major was biochemistry. She was spending summer break travelling with one of her friends. They were heading for Costa Rica. Her parents owned a ranch somewhere outside of Rocksprings. She had two sisters. She bored the shit out of me.

The only way I could remember her name was to think of Bruce Campbell from The Evil Dead movies. Ash…Ash…Ashley. It wasn't her fault. Mariela had ruined other people for me. Getting to know her was throwing yourself into the Cave of the Swallows. Getting to know anyone else was like staring at a gopher hole in the dirt.

Prince's *Te Amo Corazón* trickled from the speakers and I spun around to face the main stage. I was probably the only person in the bar who knew and loved that song. But sometimes the best stuff falls into the cracks; sometimes the sweetest sound is the sound nobody else can hear.

And there she was.

Red silk robe and black knuckle-duster heels. Her legs weapons; her body the salve to heal my aching wounds.

The dance was hypnotic. She did not move around the stage much to keep her limp hidden, but the things she could do standing on one spot blew the mind. Restriction made her creative. She swayed and rolled like a belly dancer, pushing her curves out, pulling them back in, undulating in every erotic way imaginable, the silk robe clinging to her body like a second skin, splitting just long enough to tease a glimpse of flesh before closing, healing, once again. It was like watching a butterfly in uncertain metamorphosis.

But then the robe came off, slipping from her shoulders and falling to the floor to reveal black and red panties and a peephole bra. Mariela turned her back on all of us, grabbed handfuls of her ass, gave each of us our pound of flesh. The wolves and the snakes loved it, howling and tasting the air with their tongues. In the coloured lights that stroked her skin, I saw the marks across her back that men had left behind. I saw the knuckle duster heels. I saw someone trying to take ownership of the past, a woman at war not with herself but with the things that men do.

The bar's owner, Miguel, a monster truck of a man, appeared with a beer bottle and stood it on the edge of the stage for the finale. The crowd bayed. I had seen this part of Mariela's act on the night we met – I may have even instigated it, I don't recall – but now I was ashamed to bear witness to it again. I turned away but the mirrored bar wall forced me to watch it unfold in a thousand different reflections.

Behind the bar, Ash looked sickened. She towelled a glass as if the mark would never rub off, and maybe it wouldn't. I bet she missed the home ranch now.

She saw me looking at her. Nodded across my shoulder at the stage. The baying of the crowd grew into a wave of noise poised to crush my heart and bones into dust. I was thankful when she leaned across the bar and spoke into my ear.

"He fucks all the girls," she said.

I jerked my head away from her mouth as though she had bitten a chunk from my lobe.

"What did you say?"

"That one – Miguel. He fucks them all. Perks of owning the place, I guess. He tried to fuck me the other night, but I told him I don't wanna dance so I don't wanna fuck. He got the message or went off with one of the others. Same difference."

"Wait, he doesn't…not with *all* the girls…" A drowning man will clutch at any straw to stay afloat. "What about her?" I asked.

"Who? Adrianna?"

I remembered the waitress in Aquisimon calling her by the same name right before my timely case of blowjob blindness.

Adrianna.

Twice in the space of twenty-four hours.

Fuck.

"Yeah, her," I said. "Adrianna."

"She's his favourite. He fucks her more than any of them. I don't think she even likes him that much. Maybe she just likes fucking. She sure likes beer bottles though, right?"

I bit my tongue so hard I drew blood.

"The dirty glass I gave you earlier," I said. "Where is it?"

The barmaid looked at me. "Your mouth is bleeding."

"Can I have the glass, please? I saw you put it on a tray under the bar. Hand it to me. Please, just hand it to me. The glass. Now!"

"Alright, alright," she said, and backed away in a hurry.

She looked frightened and who could blame her? Blood was running down my chin and my mouth was filling up with the stuff. I thought of copper and from that I somehow got to empty junkers rusting in a yard. Anything to keep me from thinking about Mariela and Miguel. Fuck, even their weak-ass alliteration killed me.

Junkers.

Rust.

Used.

Forgotten.

The barmaid returned with the dirty glass, the print still visible on the rim. It had a strange, slightly calming effect to hold it in my hand again, to feel the glass pressing coldly against my palm. It wasn't some obsessive-compulsive thing, although I remember being at kindergarten and building towers out of building blocks: they had to be the tallest in my class or watch out any kid who got in my way. But this was different. I needed control, yes, but this was more about the world making sense again. At that moment, I believed the glass with its dirty thumbprint had come into my life for a reason.

I spat a string-shot of blood and saliva into the bottom of the glass. Wiped my mouth with the back of my hand. Left the bar and took the glass with me. I wove between the tables on my way to the stage.

Miguel held the beer bottle above his head like a trophy, turning around so the wolves and snakes could all get a look at his prize. He brought the bottle down and held it front of his nose, then made a big show of how wonderful it smelled.

"*Salud,*" he cried, and drank long from the bottle.

I gave him the time. You let a man finish his drink. I spat another shot into my dirty glass and waited. Waited as he wiped the taste of Mariela from his lips as I had wiped the taste of blood and junkyards from mine. He turned his back to me, and I cold-cocked the motherfucker with the glass in my hand.

He fell in a heap in front of the stage. The wolves fanned out around me, silent and wary and watching. A woman screamed at the sight of all the blood on the back of Miguel's head. It was Mariela screaming; it was my blood. Some of it was his: the glass had broken, cutting his head but slicing my hand. My palm wore a smile where before it had only worn a blank look.

I wiped my hand across the front of my shirt. It left an impressive smear. The cut was deep but I wasn't going to bleed out anytime soon. Neither was Miguel, who lay face down on the floor. His legs were already moving as he started to come around. I grabbed Mariela with my good hand and pulled her off the stage. We ran toward the exit. She looked back once to check on Miguel, picked her robe up off the floor, then followed me outside.

We raced across the lot, me in front, Mariela trailing at the end of my arm, red silk robe flapping behind her like a cape, peephole bra, no panties. Men on their way into the bar stood and gawked, whooping at the free outdoor show. We reached Mariela's Nissan. Locked, no keys.

"Fuck!" I slammed the roof with my bloodied hand, leaving a stark red print on the yellow paint and sending shockwaves of pain up through my wrist and arm. The pain arrived, screaming inside my brain. I realised too late that something jagged was lodged in one of the secondary cuts on my hand and I had driven it deeper into my palm.

Mariela spun me around to face her, threw me against the car. She kissed me and grabbed me through my jeans. Deep kisses…firm, squeezing grips. My howls of pain dissolved against her lips. Blood rushed toward another part of my body. None of it was reaching my brain. I almost passed out where I stood.

A fight broke out in the lot. The wolves from the bar wanted to prevent us from leaving, while the snakes hung back and spurred them on, but the new arrivals, enjoying the free show and perhaps wanting some of the same for themselves, objected to the interference. Punches were thrown, few landed. No one really wanted to fight. But in the confusion, we slipped away and hailed a passing cab.

Mariela leaned across the front seat to instruct the driver.

"Boulevard Costero. Playa Miramar. *Vámanos!*"

"Where are we going?" I asked.

She held my gaze for a moment.

"A place I know," she said.

The driver was staring at Mariela in the rear-view mirror.

"Watch the fucking road," I said. "Mariela – where are you taking us?"

"To the beach," she said.

Where To?

"I need to get out of here," Poet said. "I can't breathe. Can we finish this outside?"

Foster shrugged. "If that's what you want. Grab your flashlight and a sidearm. Where to? Wait, no, don't answer that."

Poet nodded and followed Foster out of the cave.

There is Nothing Else to Say

It was late and Playa Miramar was all but deserted. Mariela led me to a spot away from the fire worshippers and the people out looking for crabs by flashlight, where we stood ankle-deep in the swash with our backs to the city. The full moon laid a path of brushed silver across the Gulf of Mexico as, closer to us, the surf sparkled as though filled with diamonds. We listened to the sounds of our breathing and the crashing of the waves. I remember our breathing seemed the loudest sound of all.

It was easy to see why people came to the beach at night. By day, it was crammed with sun-seekers and swimmers, families and children. But at night it was peaceful; the people spread as thin as the molecules of a gas.

Time slowed down on the beach at night, too. Conversations took twice as long, because the words only got in the way of the beautiful stretches of silence rather than the silence getting in the way of the words. Why must we fill each day with so much talk, and small talk at that? It's like releasing a thousand balloons into the air. Later, you might remember there were a lot of colours and a lot of balloons, but not much else. At night, on the beach, the talk was big, like one of those Macy's Thanksgiving Day Parade balloons. And you remember the conversation like you would remember a fifty-foot helium-filled Charlie Brown coming untied and heaving itself into the sky. But I guess there is little difference in the end. You can't hold on to a thousand or a one forever, and to remember a balloon is not the same as to feel its texture against your skin. It is a sad fact but eventually everything floats away into the altitudes of memory.

Not yet, though.

Not yet.

"What are we doing here, Mariela?"

"We had to get away," she said. "This is where I come to think."

"Is your name even Mariela?" I asked.

"What?"

"You heard me. Is that your real name? Two people in one day have called you something else. Why *is* that? Who is Adrianna?"

She laughed quietly.

"Adrianna is my – what you call it? – stage name? Sí. When I dance, when I am naked in front of the men, I am Adrianna. Mariela is the name my parents give me. It is the name I give you. It is not a lie."

"I never said it was."

"You did not have to."

"Are you fucking Miguel?"

"Yes."

I turned my head away. I could not look at her, at what she had become with that word, nor could I bear to look at the crashing surf. Those diamonds were beginning to look like pieces of broken glass. My gaze wandered farther along the beach and fell upon two men lying on a towel on the moonlit sand. Both were shirtless and wore board shorts. They were making out.

"Why?" I asked her.

"Why am I fucking him? Because he is a monster."

"That makes no sense."

"The age of consenting in my country is twelve years old," she explained. "Some of the girls who dance in the bar are young, America, very young. Not twelve but fourteen, maybe fifteen years old. They should be playing with their friends not dancing with no clothes on in front of stranger men."

"What has that got to do with you and him?"

"Miguel tries to fuck them," she said. "I keep him busy. I think if he is busy with me, he has not so much time to be busy with them. I break a little piece of the circle, sí?"

"Son of a bitch." I raged at the moon. "I knew it!"

"You want to hit me now, yes?"

I turned back to her. It hurt just looking into her eyes. My heart was baking inside my chest, the heat of humiliation spreading through me like wildfire. I felt the pain in my slashed hand beating with the rhythm of my pulse.

"Yes, I want to hit you."

"Then do it," she said.

I leaned in and kissed her forehead.

I half-expected her to cry at that. For a tear to roll down her cheek. But her eyes remained dry and the tears were mine.

I brushed them away angrily.

"I don't know why more people don't drown themselves at night," I said, staring at the Gulf. "I don't know why they don't just walk out into that water and see where it takes them. It's got to be better than slicing your wrists in a bathtub, right? Or hanging yourself in some closet somewhere because nobody knows, wants, or understands you. The water at night wants you; the water at night understands. And it knows about coldness and loneliness and going through the motions, the endless fucking motions. Jesus Christ, you fucked him, Mariela. And for what, a *good cause*? What do I even say to that?"

"I don't know."

"And there, right there – you're so matter-of-fact about it. Sometimes it's like you're dead inside." I bent and picked up a shell that lay close to my feet. Held it up. "You're like one of these, except maybe I could hear the ocean in this. If I held *you* to my ear – nothing. Not even a heartbeat." I tossed the shell back into the surf then sat on the sand just out of reach of the swash. Mariela joined me. I drew my knees up. Picked at the sand. Threw little pieces of nothing into the same sand only three feet away. "How many people have sat on this spot looking up at the moon, cursing their rotten luck, do you think? Quite a few, I expect. Do you think that's why the moon is always changing shape – because it feeds off our negative energy? It's fat, it's thin, it's fat, it's thin. It's an eating disorder in the sky. Its food is our unhappiness. I don't know what I'm saying."

"I love it when you talk like this," Mariela said, and laid a hand on my shoulder. I expected it to feel cold but it wasn't; dammit, it wasn't. "It is a little messed up. But please don't stop. Not for anyone."

I reached across my chest and laid my hand on hers.

The simple truth of it was that talking made me feel a little better. I could control words and ideas in a way that I could never control the chaos of life, of living. But it was all just blubber; a thick layer of fat against waters cold.

"I had this theory once," I said to her. "Back when I was a kid and into reading horror comics – this wasn't long after my father drove off not so much into the sunset as the moon*rise*. And this theory was that maybe all of the coldness and unhappiness we send up there is somehow siphoned back down here, only into fewer of us, so that it becomes more concentrated. Put enough unhappiness in one place, one person, and what you get is a monster, or something close to monstrous. I had this other theory too: that monsters don't want to be born, and when they realise what they are they spend the rest of their lives hating the world for it. Tell me what I should do, Mariela. You opened up to me. You told me all of this stuff about your life and then you closed the door. It's like you regret telling me any of it. How did I lose your trust? Tell me what I did, because I haven't got clue one. I'm still here. I haven't left. I'm just…waiting."

"You love me," she said.

"I have never said that."

"No…but you do."

"Well, you love me back."

"Stop putting words in my mouth. You cannot love me."

"Why?"

"Because I am no good," she said. "Because I am, how you say, *damaged good*. I have seven toes and my mind – my mind is so messed up, America. What more do you want me to say? You cannot save me. Why do you even want to try?"

"Save you?" I said. "Who wants to *save* you? I only want to hold your hand and take a run at happiness." I pointed vaguely along the beach and out, out to the deepest, darkest part of the water. "Over there. Just past the horizon and take a left. You can't see it right now but I'm telling you: it's there. Have a little faith and you'll see it in every sunrise."

I looked away from the Gulf, ashamed. It was like staring into the face of my lunatic mother after a dollar went missing from her purse. Maybe my words were lies, and maybe they were the truth. All I knew – now, as then – was what I wanted them to be.

Along the beach, the two men were still fooling around on the sand, the swash almost reaching their tangled feet. I was reminded of that famous love scene with Burt Lancaster and Deborah Kerr from the movie *From Here to Eternity*, the two of them rolling around on a beach, shrugging off the waves like they were bed sheets, as if the ocean itself could not come between them. But life wasn't like that and love wasn't like that. It was these two guys in the near-darkness, one lying on his back, arms behind his head, while the other jerked him off like he was mixing a drink. It was in the way he patiently and lovingly towelled the cum from his partner's belly when he was done and then leaned in to kiss his forehead.

So, maybe monsters were born under a full moon but something else co-existed there too: love stripped of all its pretence.

I stood and encouraged Mariela onto her feet.

"Run with me," I said. "Take my hand and run with me."

She reached for my hand and used it to pull herself onto her feet, but then she let go.

"Where?" she said. "Didn't you hear what I said? I can't leave those girls to him now. He will hurt them if I don't go back."

"Back?" I shook my head. "No, no, no. There *is* no back. You can't. Didn't you listen to yourself? You told me that I love you, and now what – you're just going to walk away from that and, and what? Go back to fucking *him*? Mariela, listen to me, please: there *is no back.*"

She shook her head and shook her head and shook her head.

"There is nowhere for us to go," she said. "I am sorry."

"But there's the whole fucking world! Choose a direction. Listen – this is not a Pi to ten digits situation here. This is *two* digits. Two. It's 3.14 and run. That's it. 3.14 and run. Let's do this. Please. Take my hand."

Then, in the darkness between our bodies, her hand found mine. Her fingertips brushed mine. Her fingers edged toward my palm just as life had crawled across that beach billions of years ago. It was epic. Monumental. I felt dizzy and swayed a little on my feet.

Mariela's face seemed to *explode* in front of me then, and pieces of it – of *her* – sprayed off to my left toward the Gulf. Her blood smacked my face like hot torrential rain, stinging my eyes, blinding me. Tiny shards of bone or shattered teeth sliced at my cheeks. The crash of the gunshot followed like a physical blow in itself, and I half ducked to one side even as I groped at my face to try and clear my sight. The taste, the smell of saltwater – or something like it – filled my mouth and clogged my nose. With what little air I had left in my lungs, that had not been stolen, I tried to clear the blockage. As I snorted and coughed and smeared her blood from my eyes, Mariela fell against me and then rolled off and onto the sand. I grabbed for her, thinking insanely that the fall might cause her an injury, but I failed to catch her in time.

I fell to my knees. Rubbed the blood from my eyes so that I could see again; not 20-20 but enough. I lifted her hand from the sand and it felt as though she was already gone. The swash reached us, dragging on Mariela's hair with its first tentative reach, encouraging her to follow as it drew back into the Gulf. The second time, the swash rolled a little farther up the beach and splashed onto her face. I saw the foam enter the brutal exit wound on her right cheek and she choked and gurgled on the mixture of saltwater and blood. She screamed against the pain but instead of a piercing sound it was muffled by the fountain of blood and water that overflowed from the ruin of her mouth. The liquids drained down her face and neck, and a small dark pool collected in the hollow of her throat. In it, I thought I glimpsed the cold reflection of the moon.

I turned to the shooter. It took a massive effort to do that, to look away from Mariela for any amount of time, because part of me thought that when I looked back she would be gone.

Miguel from the strip bar stood twenty feet away. He seemed to be in shock, looking between the lump of metal he was holding and Mariela lying stretched out on the sand, and I realised at that moment that the bullet had not been meant for her.

I launched myself at him, crossing the space separating us in no time at all. He kept looking at the smoking weapon in his hand with this hurt look, as though he could not quite believe its betrayal. The sand seemed to change from sand to something else: one of those airport conveyors, rushing me toward him. I grabbed the gun from his limp grasp. By the time his brain cleared enough to react, I had already jammed the barrel against his temple. The sack of shit fell to his knees. A dark stain bloomed on the crotch of his khaki pants. He opened his mouth to say something and I pulled the trigger and opened up his head instead. He dropped, and I moved in and knelt beside him, the gun barrel pushed deep into the hole I had just made, pulling the trigger until there were no bullets left but willing more, ten, a thousand more, into his skull.

I was screaming.

I wanted to bring him back and piece him together, just so I could kill him again.

But I had to get back to Mariela.

She was breathing but losing blood fast, and the lower half of her face was…

She was breathing.

I looked around frantically for help. The two men were gone. Their towel lay abandoned on the sand. Farther along the beach, a bunch of figures were gathered around a fire. Everybody was on their feet and looking our way, but no one moved. It was eerie, how they just stood there and watched like hyenas watching an impala drown in a lake. I spun around. There wasn't a lot of traffic on the boulevard, and what little there was – flatline: no deviation. I glanced at the sky and the stars. They never seemed so useless and small and far-away. But the moon – it looked like it was enjoying the show. Growing fat on our misery.

"GET ME SOME HELP HERE!" I yelled at the cosmos.

Then I leaned in close to Mariela so that she could see me, see that she wasn't alone.

"Baby, it's gonna be okay. We're gonna get you some help. Get you to a hospital. Get you the best doctor in the world. They'll fix you up, just like brand new, and in no time you'll be complaining about the food, okay? Okay?"

Mariela shook her head and made a gargled sound from the ruin of her mouth.

NO

A tsunami of guilt smashed into me then and sent me reeling, tumbling across the sand, clutching my head, pulling my hair. I sat up in a foetal position, rocking on my heels, looking askance at Mariela through the frame created by my bent right arm and my palm rubbing hard on the top of my skull.

She was right. She deserved better than empty promises and soft clichés.

"I'm sorry," I said, and dragged the rest of me back through the sand to her side. I took her hand in mine. She tried to squeeze my fingers, but her grip was weaker even than my words.

Then the shaking of her head changed to a nod, and her eyes widened a fraction but fixed on me with intent.

"No," I said.

Nod.

"There's no way… I love you. I *can't.*"

Her eyes beseeched mine.

YES

I reached out and held her head in place so that she could not do it, could not nod at me again. But beneath my grip there was the tiniest transference of kinetic energy, and without her head visibly moving I felt it happen again.

I lost it.

"Fuck you," I said, then across my shoulder, screaming into the dark: "SOMEONE CALL 911!

SHE'S BEEN SHOT. SHE'S BLEEDING. CALL 911!" And then to Mariela: "It was Miguel. He did this. He meant to kill me, but…how – how did he know where to find us?"

From somewhere in her blood-drowning throat she made another gurgling sound.

One word.

Incomprehensible.

"How did he know, Mariela?"

And there she was in my mind: the waitress with the paper coasters and the smile like a flickering motel sign.

Don't go to the beach… She takes them all to the beach.

"Mariela… Mariela…"

It was all I could say, over and over: the way a child will repeat a thing they so desperately want to be true.

A nod.

Eyes rolled back. White as moons.

YES

And I placed my hands around her neck and pressed my thumbs hard and deep into the throat I had kissed, loved.

YES

Afterwards, I swear she parted her lips to speak again. Blood frothed from her mouth and the hole in her face. Maybe she wasn't… I don't know. But I leaned in close to hear what she had to say.

Three words. Or maybe not so much words as expelled air that carried a sound, like the whisper of dead leaves on the wind.

Nearly a decade later, on a beach in northern Libya, Poet and Foster stood in the beams of each other's Maglites. Foster felt cold fingers climbing the ladder of his spine. He shivered, and swept his flashlight around in a full circle, half-expecting some leering, putrescent insult to humanity to stumble out of the darkness into the cone of light. Or was it half-hoping? His pistol safety was off, and he thought that pulling the trigger and sending a bullet into *something* seemed the perfect antidote to his unease. Listening to Poet talk about Mariela made him think of the woman *he* had loved. Carol. In a world of hidden corners, she was around every one. But she was dead to him: she was not coming back; he could never allow it. As for Poet…Foster saw him as some pathetic swine visiting a trough of poisoned water and yet forced to drink by his own unslakeable thirst.

Poor bastard, he thought.

"What happened next?" he asked.

"I walked into the Gulf," Poet said. "I wanted to drown myself but something wouldn't let me do it. I waded out to my waist and looked down. I still had the gun in my hand, but there were no bullets left. I threw it as far as I could and waited for the splash, but it never came. It must have been swallowed by the waves. And that's when I realised I couldn't do it. I had a kid on the way. A slow train that would hit me in five months. At least my father had stuck around for a little while before he left us. I couldn't do it. So I ran from the beach, took a cab back to Mariela's place, gathered my stuff, and split that same night. I hitchhiked all the way back to Galveston and Angela. Then I waited for the knock on the door. Like the gun and the splash, it was supposed to happen, but it never came. The Mexican cops must have decided they had their killer. There were witnesses, I knew that much, but what I didn't know was whether or not any of them had come forward. The two guys fooling around on the towel – maybe they weren't, you know, *out*, and maybe one or both of them had a wife at home. The people around the fire – I thought some of them might come forward, but maybe nobody wanted to get involved and the beach was clear before the cops even showed up. I don't know. But just because they never knocked didn't mean I could stop running. So four months later, I enlisted."

"And here you are on a beach reliving the whole thing."

"Here I am."

Poet felt relieved that he had finally told his story, and yet he felt worse for it: the hole inside him now completely uncovered and exposed. He realised that it had been filled all these years with the words of its own telling. A makeshift grave. And now that the past was no longer buried, the dead were free to roam.

"I'm tired of running," he said. "It only takes me farther from her. Her face has faded so much…and when I see it I only see what that bullet did to her. I can see her foot and her missing toes and the ankle tattoo above it, but her face? It's fading. You know, it was years later that I realised what that tattoo actually meant – the feather and the barbs breaking off and transforming into birds…swallows. It meant 'birds of a feather.' How could I have not seen that? I mean, think about the sacrifices she made for those young girls in the bar and it makes perfect sense. That's what it means. And I know I heard her say those words to me with her last breath. I know she said those words."

"So tell me what she said."

"I can't."

"Why not?"

"Because it's between me and her," Poet said. He tried to shrug it off, but in the unblinking glare of Foster's Maglite his face betrayed his full torment at the memory. "There is nothing else to say."

Foster nodded. It was time to shut this down.

"You know she didn't actually say anything, right? She was already gone by that point."

"Maybe," Poet said. "Maybe not."

Foster was reminded of an adolescent tugging the petals from a flower. *She loves me, she loves me not. She loves me…*

"Truth is: she didn't love you at all. She didn't want your love. But she got it anyway, didn't she? Sounds like our foreign policy, son. You're in the right place."

"I didn't imagine it. She spoke to me. She said three words – *those* three words."

"And I believe you believe that."

"Haven't you been *listening*? It's not all in my mind."

"Oh, I've been listening to every word," Foster said. "But the song I've been listening to is Leonard Cohen. The one *you're* hearing is Whitney Houston. They're not the same. Not the same at all."

"No. You're wrong. I was there."

"Son, listen. Between me, you, and the Mediterranean, I have done things. Things of which I am in no way proud. I have put down dying men, enemy soldiers disembowelled by our air strikes and left lying out on the hot sand, literally holding in their own guts. No medical aid nearby. Not even the enemy anymore but soldiers, men, just like us. I've ended them. And even after a bullet stopped their heart I heard them talk to me – in here." Foster tapped his chest. "And in here." His skull. "The dead like to have the final word and usually they get it. But what you gotta realise is it's us doing the talking. It's *all* us."

Poet lowered his right hand holding the Maglite, and with it reached for the bandage on his left. Foster vanished into the darkness behind the glare of his own flashlight.

The wound underneath the bandage was the only physical reminder of his time with Mariela. The kisses, the fucking, they faded: too quickly, it seemed sometimes; other times, not quickly enough. But you could drown kisses and sex in a sea of kisses and sex. That was the easy part. The pain faded too, in time, replaced by a numb longing for the very thing you lost: pain, feeling, *life*. Only scars endured. Scars were the doors to the past, albeit sealed shut. Sometimes you had to open them. To remind yourself you were not one of them.

The dead.

The *un*dead.

Poet remembered standing over the body of the girl on the beach.

The Girl from Yesterday.

Mariela.

Remembered looking down at where her face used to be, now little more than a bloody ruin framed by long, blood-soaked Mediterranean—

Mexican

—hair.

When there was no face, you forgot what she had looked like when she had one.

When there was no face, you could make her look like anyone you wanted.

He remembered tracing the tip of his boot knife along the old scar on his left hand and thinking—

Enough…
Blood.
Enough…
Pain.
Enough.
He unravelled the bandage from his hand and tossed it into the flames, where it flared into a ribbon of fire for a few moments and then resigned itself to the process of burning.

"I never wanted to tell this story," he said to Foster, looking at him now and really seeing him for the first time since finishing the tale. "Part of me hates telling it. But then, it brings her back, and that I don't mind; that I like. The thing is – and I was clear on this from the beginning – Mariela? She dies in the end. She *always* dies in the end. And I can't keep losing her. I need to take it back."

"Coffey style," Foster said.

"That's right." Poet smiled sadly. "'Like the drink but spelled different'."

"But he couldn't do it in the end."

"What?"

"He tried but he couldn't. Sometimes it really is too late. You can't change the past. You can't even rewrite it. Believe me, I've tried."

"No, but what you can do is tell it again – fresh."

"It's a tragic story, son, and I truly wish there was something I could say that could change the outcome for you. But you said it yourself: words don't help. Stories don't change a thing in the end, no matter how many times you tell them."

"I need to—"

"Take it back, I know," Foster said. "I know. But don't do it."

"Great stories are like great songs," Poet said. "They carry you away and then they bring you back. But the *truly* great ones change you in small ways every time you hear them – and every time you hear them feels like the first time."

"Don't do it, son."

"Stop talking."

"I can't," Foster said, tears in his eyes. "Because as long as I do I figure you won't pull the trigger. Words matter to you, right? Stories matter. Let me tell you *my* story. The reason I stay out here, why I haven't walked away from all of this and just gone home to my daughters – I have four daughters, Poet – it's so I can tell myself Carol is still there. At home. With them. It's so I can tell myself she's still my wife. That she doesn't drink too much. That she never reversed our SUV over a two-year-old boy standing in our driveway. Or that the two-year-old boy wasn't our only son. But home is nothing but a lie and Carol belongs to the worms. So let's say Mariela loved you. In her own way, maybe she did. But it seems to me she was running from the truth. Just like me. And just like you right now. Because that is what we do, as people, as nations, as a fucking species the whole world over. We save ourselves with fictions. Well, here's some *non*-fiction for you, asshole: she didn't love you. She never loved you. She screwed you over. Just like *I* screwed you over. See, everything I've told you is a lie. Just like everything *she* told you. Every night, on my watch, I've been letting them through. That's right. I've been taking my finger out of the dam while you've been counting sheep, and by now Julius has spread halfway across the Middle East, and who knows, maybe even farther than that. But it's a beautiful possibility, don't you think? I mean, who are you gonna tell your story to when there's no one left to tell?"

"You're lying," Poet said.

"Are you sure about that?" Foster said. "I mean, as sure as you are about, say, Mariela?"

"Are you finished?"

"No, I got one more thing for you."

"What is it?"

"There is nothing else to say."

The bullet entered Foster's skull through his right eye. He fell backwards, twitching, onto the sand and rocks as the gunshot rolled out across the Mediterranean. Poet turned to follow the sound. After a few seconds it was gone and there were only the waves labouring to wash the world clean as they had always done and always would. He focussed on the waves.

Using his Maglite, he gathered driftwood and arranged it on the sand close to Foster's body. Soon, a small fire burned on the beach, one tiny voice singing against the dark and dissonant chorus of the sea. He pulled the accelerant from his waistband and squirted Foster's body with the odorous liquid until the can wheezed emptily. He lifted Foster's legs and dragged his body closer to the fire then dropped his legs into the flames. The accelerant on his boots caught and the flames spread rapidly up the rest of his body.

Foster's sidearm lay on the sand close to his hand. Poet ducked and dragged it out of the reach of the fire. He checked the safety was engaged. It was. He pushed the gun into his waistband. Walked away from the beach.

On the path to the cave, he found the undead terrorist still tied to a rock. It lay on its back in a stinking, hot pool of its own gore, armless, legless, intent on walking the air with its stumps, looking for any purchase at all, like a cockroach on its back. When the bullet entered its brain there was no twitching, no fight, only a sudden and final cessation of movement. Either death was a disappointment or the terrorist had loitered so long in its garden it was just like going home.

Or going nowhere at all, Poet thought.

He headed back to the cave. Above him, the sky was dark and low, like a black shroud pulled tight across the face of the world. His lungs hurt when he breathed. The pain in his hand sang to the beat of his pulse, echoing down through the years from the car park outside *La Señoras Locas* in Mexico and from the beach behind him just days past, when standing over the body of the Maltese girl he had reopened the wound with his knife. Only, the beach would never be behind him. There would always be another beach, another incarnation of Mariela in his future. Pain was an addiction, even if you never felt it; maybe more so. The story may be untold and the words taken back, but they itched to be worked loose again, like phantom slivers of glass trapped inside the flesh of his palm.

Except there are no slivers and the pain is phantom and Foster was right: *it's all us*, he thought. Everything is a lie. We are twisted walking fictions and the truth only reaches our slow, addled brains by The End. The world is full of monsters. Let them eat the world. Let *us* eat it.

He glanced up at the sky. The full moon loomed particularly large. Practically engorged.

Walking, he looked at the stars. They shone clearly tonight. The night sky invariably reminded him of

Mariela's smooth skin, the stars those tiny welts of old scars, past hurts, across her back. When even the sky delivered her to him, he realised there really was no escape. She was part of his firmament now. The night breeze blew warmly on his face, carrying with it the faint perfume of flowers, tickling his senses and firing memories inside his brain like flares lighting up the dark for a moment before fading, falling into the black. And there: a shooting star. A satellite or a comet. Or maybe a high altitude ballistic missile, carrying another payload of Julius somewhere. It came out of the north, sliding over his head and across the sky toward the south, tracing a path down the length of Mariela's spine. The tips of his fingers tingled at the memory of touching those tiny ridges of bone through her skin. Like reading a beautiful sentence in Braille. He smiled as tears began to blur his vision and his gaze returned to ground level.

Is this what it feels like to be a monster? he wondered. *Because I thought – I thought it would be more.*

On the hillside up ahead, he saw the cave by moonlight, he saw the broken fence that ran in front of its mouth and along the path that led back down to the beach. He saw the white, leaning board signs with their warnings written in red Arabic. And he saw, all around him, the pale flowers of the asphodel meadow gathered like ghosts, poised and waiting.

Holding their final breath.

Steven J Dines writes fiction of a dark, psychological persuasion, be it horror, fantasy, crime, or mainstream. His short fiction has appeared in publications such as *Black Static* (nine times), *Interzone* (twice), *Crimewave*, *Fireside Magazine*, and many others. Originally from Aberdeen, Scotland, he now lives south of the border in Salisbury with his wife, Summer, and their two sons, Joshua and Taylor.

www.ingramcontent.com/pod-product-compliance
Lightning Source LLC
Chambersburg PA
CBHW030805190726
48285CB00003B/1037